The Headhunter

Not everything is what it seems

By Spencer D Hawkes

Dedicated to 'Bird'. Fly high, fly straight, fly far.

Street Press
London

Copyright © 2025 by Spencer D. Hawkes

The moral right of the author is hereby asserted in accordance with The Copyright, Designs and Patents Act 1988.

All characters and events in this publication, other than those clearly in the public domain, are fictitious and any resemblance to actual persons, living or dead, is purely coincidental.

All rights reserved. No part of this publication may be reproduced, stored in a retrieval system, or transmitted, in any form or by any means without the prior written permission of the publisher, nor be otherwise circulated in any form of binding or cover other than that in which it is published and without a similar condition being imposed on the subsequent buyer.

A CIP catalogue record for this book is available from the British Library.

ISBN 9798291259054
Typeset by Abdul Rehman
Cover design by Street Press

Foreword

In *The Postmaster General,* Spencer D. Hawkes introduced the world to Ian Taylor – a man who shuffled, drank and snacked his way through a series of increasingly perilous assignments with shambolic charm, low animal cunning, and a metabolic rate that baffled medical science. Between the polite façades of suburban life and the high-stakes shadows of international espionage, Ian emerged improbably victorious, if not entirely fragrant.

Now, in *The Headhunter*, Ian returns – slightly promoted, marginally upgraded, and still spectacularly unwashed. His new Post Office title, "Philatelic Ambassador," grants him the perfect cover to roam the globe, flitting between international stamp expos and symposia, while quietly carrying out surgical eliminations on behalf of MI5 and a rotating cast of intelligence services so secret that even they deny their own existence.

This time, the threats are bigger, the targets slipperier, and the hotel breakfast buffets truly baroque. And somewhere, in the shadows of it all, Malcolm Duffy – Ian's nemesis, who escaped capture last time round – is circling once more, not merely seeking revenge, but something far more personal.

There will be death. There will be deception. There will be a diplomatic incident at a luxury hotel in Geneva involving cheese with its own heraldry, sausages of glistening menace, and a waffle station with more strategic nuance than a NATO summit.

"The buffet stretched the length of the room. A living altar to cholesterol and culinary brinkmanship. Ian approached like a man possessed. What followed was an act of gastronomic violence the hotel would later refer to simply as 'The Incident.'"

Packed with dry wit, breakfast diplomacy, and savage takedowns both bureaucratic and ballistic, The Headhunter is a darkly funny spy thriller about identity, obsolescence, and trying to keep your head... while everyone around you is losing theirs.

Ian Taylor is a contradiction. Equal parts lethal and ludicrous. He moves between family dinners and global manhunts, low-cost mailings at work and off-book executions – all while dreaming not of medals or martyrdom, but of *fondue moitié-moitié truffée à la royale*, garnished with white Alba truffle, wagyu charcuterie, and a 1960s Fendant, chilled to near-religious perfection.

Ian Taylor doesn't strut. But he does deliver.

And this time, he's back to finish what he started – on a world stage where everything is at stake, and the coffee rarely has enough sugar.

Contents

Chapter 1
First Class Travel — 11

Chapter 2
The Geneva Convention — 35

Chapter 3
Vienna Waltz — 59

Chapter 4
The Queen's Penny — 79

Chapter 5
Singapore Sling — 93

Chapter 6
The Librarian — 109

Chapter 7
Return to Sender — 117

Chapter 8
Don't Lose Your Head — 145

Chapter 9
All Good Things Come to an End — 161

Chapter 10
The Long Shot — 177

Chapter 11
Outside, a Barn Owl Hooted — 189

Chapter One
First Class Travel

"Never trust a man who alphabetises his condiments."
~ MI6 Psychological Profiling Brief (Redacted)

Chapter 1
First Class Travel

It began, as so many of Ian Taylor's days did, with an act of early morning culinary vandalism. At 7:08 a.m., the kitchen of his North London home resembled a war zone in a Bombay street market. Ian stood barefoot in sagging grey boxers, open fronted tartan dressing gown, and a very old, moth eaten "I Visited Ipswich" t-shirt. He ladled piping hot chicken tikka masala onto a plate already sporting two badly fried eggs – snotty yet somehow at the same time burnt. The thick curry sauce sploshed over them with abandon, running like lava across the ceramic plate and pooling into four slices of fried bread on the side. He sniffed it appreciatively, cracked open a can of Lilt, took a swig, and belched loudly.

Max, his Son, walked in and stopped dead.

"Jesus Christ, Dad. It's not even eight. What happened to cornflakes or a healthy option?"

"Cornflakes," Ian said theatrically, without turning, "are for men who've given up on life. Men who spend their time at endless Tupperware parties and crochet evenings."

Max stared. "You smell like a bin at a petrol station."

"Thank you," Ian said proudly, spooning further curry over the eggs with remarkable precision. "A man must find joy where he can."

"Are you actually planning to go to work like that?" asked Max looking at his Dad's eclectic, stain spattered clothing.

"Well, I'm not doing this for fashion, Maximus. This is art."

Max retreated, muttering something about calling Social Services or better still Care in the Community. Ian sat at the kitchen table with the stubborn dignity of a man defending the final hill in a battle, curry cascading down his hand and onto his dressing gown and then onto the dog.

Tolstoy, his vast Russian Black Terrier curled under the table, let out a single approving grunt as the sauce trickled onto the floor and his back. He licked up what he could reach appreciatively.

Susan, Ian's long-suffering Wife, wearing an expression last seen on a vicar's face witnessing the second coming of Satan, slid past with a mug of fennel tea and a crystal tucked under her bra strap for 'balance.'

"Daddy," she said, not looking at him, "you're leaking curry onto the dog."

"He doesn't mind Mummy. He sees it as a great treat," Ian said emphatically, feeding Tolstoy a long strip of naan bread. He then mopped up some of the bright red sauce from the dog's back with another strip of the bread and ate it, hairs and all, with satisfaction. Susan turned away with a noise somewhere between an exasperated sigh and a loud choke.

"And don't forget to take the bins out. And the recycling. And make sure you take your cholesterol tablet this morning;

you keep forgetting it. And it looks like you might need it with what you are eating for breakfast, for heaven's sake," she went on.

Ian wiped his mouth on a tea towel already hosting an alarming gravy shadow from the night before and began assembling himself ready for the day. A pair of trousers last seen at a 1990s garden party, a shirt with one collar point permanently bent outwards, and socks of such advanced vintage that the heels had become non-existent. The back of his shoes had been trodden flat into a kind of clog, a defiant gesture against modern footwear standards.

By 8:05, Ian was on the move. He stank to high heaven, not having had a bath or shower. That and the fact he had gorged on an incredibly smelly curry with fried eggs for breakfast. He shuffled towards the train station in a fog of cumin, paprika and faint egg. He nodded at Mrs Patel at the end of his street who was hosing down her front step and avoided eye contact with a neighbour whose name he couldn't remember but who always said "Morning" with the passive aggression of a man awaiting a neighbourhood parking dispute. The street, in this part of leafy North London, was lined with perfectly clipped hedges, polished Volvos, and houses with names like "Hazelbank" and "Lavender Nook." Ian's house, of course, had no name. But it did have a squeaky gate and a wisteria that hadn't been properly pruned since 2012.

As he walked down the road towards the railway station, he saw what looked like a very large bird perched on the metal fencing that kept the public off the railway tracks. Ian thought he must be hallucinating or something. Perhaps it was the effect of too much curry so early in the morning, or too much Scotch the day before.

As he got closer, he realised it was an enormous bird of prey!

"It's an omen," he muttered loudly – to no one in particular. As he came up opposite, on the other side of the road, he realised it was something like a Golden Eagle. Ian rubbed his eyes. But when he looked again the bird was still there. The Eagle then soared off in a great arc into the sky. Ian looked at an equally shocked commuter who was passing and said, "you know the Romans saw the sighting of an eagle as a sign of future victory, of great change and glory." The man now becoming slightly alarmed at this bizarre turn of events, scuttled off at great pace, like a small mouse or shrew. First a large eagle on the way to work, now an even larger scruffy, smelly man spouting strange proclamations, breathing curry all over him.

"To glory," Ian announced loudly, scaring two Lycra clad Millennials, also on their way to the station. He then took off at pace after the small shrew like man ahead of him.

The station was its usual combination of crumbling Victorian gloom and pigeon guano. It never changed. Each day blended into the next, although Ian had to quietly admit to himself today that it was a turn up for the books to see a large eagle on the station railings. Ian descended into the tiled underworld of the station like a large waddling mole – belching and farting curry in rhythm as he went.

On the train, he was wedged between a man with active dandruff and a woman eating a fruit salad with sociopathic intensity. Opposite, a young girl was doing her make-up with surgical focus, flicking fragments of make up over the elderly woman sitting next to her. His mind drifted between the soft bubbling of the chicken tikka masala and egg breakfast in his stomach and a vague sense of existential dread. He then farted – silently but deadly, engulfing the entire carriage with the dark smell of death.

He pretended he hadn't noticed the smell and got up to escape, then tutted in a theatrical manner at an old man near the door – pretending it was him who had created the offensive stench. Ian then quickly moved to the next carriage – hoping the appalling smell hadn't followed him.

Ian sat between a man reading about cryptocurrency and a woman loudly shaming her boyfriend on her mobile phone for not remembering their two-week anniversary. Opposite him, a girl applied mascara using the train window as a mirror, nearly gouging her eye out every time the train hit a bump.

Ian stared at his own reflection in the window. He looked like a man who had overslept during a great storm and then walked in from the sea. Hair like old Velcro. Shirt from the bin. Tie? Absent. Confidence? Surprisingly present.

30 minutes later, Ian arrived at Kings Cross and shuffled out through the ticket hall and struggled up the stairs to the big station concourse – where tramps and buskers jockeyed for position. He sped along the glass fronted area of the station, swigging whisky from a hip flask, as he tore towards his place of work – Post Office Headquarters, where he was a mid-level marketing manager. He managed

all the organisation's legal and regulatory communications to customers – price increases, the withdrawal of a service, that kind of thing.

He walked out into the urban jungle of the surrounding streets, hiccupping curry fumes and now whisky. He walked with purpose – like a man late for a parole hearing – towards his office. But first, some further sustenance he thought.

Once he hit the junction of Euston Road and Pentonville Road, he pulled out his trusty hip flask once again and continued to swig at the whisky inside. He veered right into Kings Cross Road, stopping at a local shop near to the Prince Albert Public House on Acton Street to buy several family-sized bags of salt and vinegar crisps, two low-grade sandwiches, full of egg mayonnaise and factory produced culinary despair. He also decided to order two sausage rolls and a coffee the temperature of magma for good measure. He struggled to carry it all dropping the sandwiches in their cheap carboard packets on the floor twice as he tried to pay. The man behind the counter looked like he'd once auditioned for a zombie film and hadn't needed makeup.

"A man's got to keep his strength up," he muttered to the shop owner, biting into a packet of salt and vinegar crisps to open it, like it owed him money.

He walked fast in a focused yet slightly erratic way until he arrived at Post Office Head Office – an angular, eclectic mix of glass, steel, wrapped around 1930s Art Deco architecture - complete with potted plants no one watered and a security system no one trusted or respected. The receptionists smiled at Ian as he entered, as did the security guards, one of whom even gave Ian a small wave.

The Headhunter

They'd long stopped asking long ago why he didn't come into the office regularly like everyone else. But Ian had his own peculiar rhythms and friends in strange places. And anyway, they liked Ian. He was about the only person who stopped to talk to them, to ask them about their lives.

Ian squeezed through the security barrier with a small apologetic belch, leaving a faint aura of turmeric in his wake. He found an empty desk on the first floor and clumsily knocked a half-filled plastic cup of water all over a stack of out-of-date tariff letters as he sat down. Ian dabbed at the spillage with some of the discarded letters, trying to mop it up quickly without having to go to the kitchen for paper napkins.

It was then that his boss Ruth emerged from her slightly smarter than everyone else's glass-fronted office. She was waving an expensive looking pen – probably a Cartier, Ian thought – in her hand like a magic wand. She beckoned him with the air of a woman summoning a plumber to discuss a blocked u-bend.

"Is that a Cartier," Ian asked, aligning his eyes about inch away from her fancy pen, staring at it in mock awe. Ruth snatched the pen away from where Ian stood and hid it behind her back looking slightly panicked by his eccentric behaviour.

Ruth wore a sharp tweed suit in muted colours and wielded sarcasm like a rapier. Her dark hair was formed into an immaculate ponytail, her voice sharp and crisp very much like a BBC announcer on sedatives. Yet Ian made her feel very uneasy.

"Ian," she said, tone flat as a steamrolled sandwich, "can we have a quick chat in my office please." Ian didn't like the sound of this. This kind of request normally ended with Ian being given more work and ending up with less time to manage his 'other work'.

She waved him into her office with all the enthusiasm of someone inviting a raccoon to a wedding.

He walked into Ruth's office, and she shut the door abruptly behind them both.

"I saw a Golden Eagle this morning on the way to work," Ian blurted out, trying to deflect whatever Ruth wanted to share with him so badly.

Ruth looked at Ian with a distant mildly confused air. "Yes, everyone has, half of England, it's been on the TV news this morning. They think it might have escaped from a zoo in Bristol or something." She confirmed irritably.

"It might be an omen of great change, or impending victory," Ian continued helpfully. "The Romans you know…" he started.

"Well, I am glad to hear it." Ruth replied, Cutting him off abruptly. She didn't have patience this morning for Ian's nonsense. "In fact there are going to be some big changes… we're making some team changes."

"Changes?" he said, halfway through eating a chewable vitamin C tablet that had been in his jacket pocket since about 2017. It was the closest thing that Ian had to an indigestion tablet, and he was beginning to suffer from starting the day with eggs a la chicken tikka masala! He hoped it might do the trick, although he somehow doubted it.

"A lateral move. You'll be joining Philatelic Products. As a Philatelic Ambassador"

Ian blinked. "Stamp collecting? Bloody stamp collecting? Stamps and collectibles?"

"Stamps, commemoratives, collectibles. You'll also be editor-in-chief of the Stamp Collectors Bulletin."

"Oh good. That sounds... tedious," moaned Ian.

She ignored him. "It's an international publication with a huge global subscriber base. You'll be representing us at lots of international events in Geneva, Vienna, Singapore and Brussels. You name it you can go there. Smart hotels, lots of nice food," she added trying to make it seem attractive.

Ian's jaw shifted gears mid-chew.

"Geneva, you say?" asked Ian.

"Your itinerary for the first few months is in your inbox. But after that you can set your own agenda... within reason," she added cautiously – nervous that Ian may take advantage if encouraged too much.

Ian stood very still. Then slowly, like a bear spotting salmon in the river, or fine honey in the meadow, he nodded.

"Well. This is quite the promotion."

She gave him a long look. "Frankly, Ian, it gets you out of the office and off my carpet. And hopefully HR will finally stop asking me why you are never in. It's a win, win all round."

Ian returned to his desk and pulled out his 'secret' encrypted phone from his curry-stained trousers. He quickly walked to the toilets and locked himself in a cubicle.

His stomach grumbled. The tikka masala was staging a rebellion. He farted so loudly it rattled the toilet door.

Ian sent a message to Griffin – his MI5 handler: *Change of situation. International opportunity. Need to meet today. Laundrette. What time today is good?*

Reply: *1400. Bring coins – I need to do my towels.*

Ian looked up at the inside of the toilet cubical door to see a cheaply made laminated sign he hadn't spotted before.

It read *'Please leave the toilet in the condition you would wish to find them. Using the loo brush where required.'*

Ian laughed. "They won't want to be doing any of that after I've jettisoned my chicken tikka egg supreme in here," he muttered, slightly missing the point that you were supposed to tidy up after yourself.

It could be dangerous work being a Post Office worker – particularly for the cleaners of the office toilets, Ian mused.

Ian sat at his desk and booted up his ancient laptop. It wheezed into life like a pensioner being asked to dance. Ian checked his itinerary for his new role and searched online for a few of the hotels that had been booked for him, wondering if Griffin could get him an upgrade or two – perhaps a Presidential Suite, with posh snacks and a minibar. Maybe even some club class travel to ease the executive stress of it all.

Ian scrolled through the agenda. Keynote speeches. Collector showcases. Gala dinners. Black tie events. Ian made a note: buy tuxedo – or maybe try to borrow one from Griffin.

Before long, it was time for him to set off for the City to meet with Griffin, at their usual secret rendezvous – a seedy, run down launderette just off the City Road on the way to Bank Station.

The walk to the launderette was brisk. Ian passed two suited City gents chatting animatedly outside a sushi bar, their hands flapping like over-caffeinated sparrows. He gave them a sidelong glance, suspicious, then dipped into a newsagent to buy a bottle of cheap brandy in a plastic bottle – to help keep his strength up. He walked past a busy Turkish barber shop, the barbers were wrapping hot towels around customers faces, sharpening their razors on leather belts ready to shave these City boys to within a millimetre of their designer suited lives. Turkish barbers and cafes, *The epicentre of Albanian money laundering operations these days, Ian tutted to himself.*

And then he spotted a small Indian Restaurant (The Curry Leaf), he'd been there before, *Tempting... But enough*, thought Ian. He'd had quite enough Indian food for one day.

In the corner of his eye, for a split second, Ian thought he saw a large bird circling in the sky above the City. Above him. He blinked and looked again but there was nothing. He was probably just imagining it.

At 2:00 p.m. sharp, Ian entered the dark, dusty launderette he and Griffin often met in. It smelled of damp socks, industrial soap and homeless people. Griffin, ex-Gurkha, was folding clean towels like they'd committed serious crimes against humanity – across several global time zones. Small, compact, and built like granite, Griffin had eyes like polished stone and a voice that suggested he could kill you with a flick of a highly starched cotton towel.

The launderette was humid, it was grim, and Griffin stood in front of a row of spinning machines like a monk conducting a washing ritual. Griffin nodded. Ian nodded back. They spoke in code, mostly about washing powders and softener preferences, but the message was clear: this was serious.

"You smell like a Bombay brothel," Griffin said laughing.

"Thank you," Ian said. "I try my best."

"There are going to be some big changes at the Post Office," Ian stuttered. "I'm being moved to stamps."

"What does that mean?" asked Griffin.

Ian explained that he was going to work on collectible stamps, and that this meant he would be able to travel across Europe – more or less at will, to any location there was a stamp collection fair or convention – or where 'they' (MI5, or any one of about a dozen other covert organisations) needed a quick assassination or undercover operation undertaken.

"Philately, doesn't that involve you using your tongue or something," joked Griffin suggestively? "Well, you can certainly lick some stamps," joked Ian, "These days you can even lick King Charles's backside if you want – assuming they are gummed!"

Griffin pulled a face of mock disgust and horror.

Ian handed over a copy of his itinerary. Griffin gave it a cursory glance.

Griffin raised one thick eyebrow. "That... actually works. We've got a lot of wet work all over Europe and Asia and who would suspect a bloody stamp collector. It's just so boring!" He laughed a deep chugging laugh.

"Geneva. Vienna. Singapore. Stamp fairs and Symposiums. Provides you with perfect cover," continued Griffin.

"I got some other news this morning," said Griffin. "An encrypted update came in. Mr Duffy and his large bear like sidekick may have been spotted in Vienna. We are investigating further."

Griffin folded another towel with dangerous precision. "Might be your chance to finish him off once and for all."

Malcolm Duffy. For Ian, the name hung like dense fog. A soft-voiced man with a sweater vest, a ridiculous collection of Staffordshire ceramic dogs, and an unsettling knack for disappearing when you least expected it. Ian had watched him for days from his wet back garden. They'd played hedge-to-hedge surveillance chicken for over a week. And then Duffy had simply vanished, leaving behind nothing but a shattered porcelain spaniel full of military grade explosives and an endless trail of misdirection. But now? He was back on their radar. And Vienna was calling.

Ian and Griffin finished their discussion and Ian waddled off in the direction of his secret luxury Penthouse apartment hidden deep in the City.

The Penthouse was Ian's secret bolt-hole. The building was the perfect place to relax, stay hidden and change into a disguise when he needed to, with a private lift that knew his fingerprints. The penthouse itself was silent perfection: hardwood floors, minimalist furniture, a humidor of vintage cigars, and a mirrored wall that slid open to reveal weapons, passports, wigs, and all the latest untraceable tech. His suits were custom made – with designer labels. The shoes made from the finest Italian leather. The whisky older than his children. From here, Ian ran the other half of his life – the secret half – with careful, ruthless precision. There were weapons and explosives hidden away here, where every fitment flipped to reveal an arsenal of gadgetry à la Tracey Island.

He stared out across the city skyline, swirling a glass of 30-year-old Glenmorangie, then keyed in several new messages to his MI5 handlers. Logistics. He needed cover stories. Reservations. He could stay where Post Office had booked him in – but it would make him a potential target he had argued. A better room or hotel would help with security he claimed. Private entrances, maybe someone to watch his room during the day, while he was working. The wheels turned quickly when oiled by whisky and a new cover story with an International dimension. Everything slotted into place with the efficiency of a well-packed suitcase full of high-powered weaponry.

By the time the sky turned a soft amber, and the streets below glowed with the desperation of commuters heading home, Ian was already back on the Northern Line, weaving through the crowds like a mildly drunk eel. The train stank of wet coats, baked humanity, and cheap perfume. Ian didn't mind. He was distracted. His mind buzzed with images: his latest target's dossier, the cool marble lobby of a smart Swiss hotel. Geneva. Precision. Neutrality. And an assassination – with a sticky ending.

Back in leafy North London, he let himself into his house with the quiet shuffle of a man trying not to attract too much attention. The door stuck slightly, as always. Tolstoy greeted him with a thud of his great tail against the hallway radiator. Susan was in the kitchen, humming to herself as she sprinkled dried oregano into a shepherd's pie. A large crystal sat on the kitchen worktop, catching the early evening glow. The house smelled of lamb, potato and herbs, with a slight undercurrent of dog.

"Evening, Mummy," Ian said, pecking her cheek.

"You're very chipper tonight," she said, eyeing him. "Have you been drinking or something?"

"No. Well, just a cheeky one on the way home. I got a promotion today. I'm basically Royal Mail royalty now. I'm a philatelic ambassador."

"That's not a word."

"It is now!"

She looked unconvinced. "You? Really? Promoted? Not a mistake? They do know who you are, don't they?"

"Apparently I'm the new editor of the Post Office's Stamp Collector's Bulletin. Stamp stuff. International events. I'll be travelling. Europe mostly."

She blinked and stuttered, surprised... turning into mild alarm at the very thought. "You? Travelling?"

Max and Daisy both appeared in the doorway like summoned spirits. Daisy, Ian's Daughter, was in her yoga leggings and a designer hoodie, smart, wafer thin, laptop under one arm and disapproval already all over her face.

"Did you say 'stamps Dad'? she said. That... just about sums you up. Bland, boring, and irrelevant. People don't even send letters anymore."

Ian grinned. "Thank you, darling. Glad you are pleased for me."

Max leaned against the fridge. "Wait, travelling? Like, abroad? How often?"

"Few days every month I would think," Ian shrugged. "Maybe more. Depends how long each event is."

Susan narrowed her eyes. "They won't let you near any rare or valuable stamps, will they Daddy?" the alarm in her voice increasing.

Ian gave his most innocent smile. "No, I'll just be shaking hands with boring stamp collectors Mummy. Admiring perforations and the colour palette of certain stamps."

"Well, I guess you aren't likely to get into too much trouble mixing with lots of old, boring stamp collectors," said Susan.

That night, Ian slurped the shepherd's pie down like a man attempting to inhale it through his eyebrows. He had decided to eat it with a side of thick French Fries (arguing a need for double carbs!). Susan watched him suspiciously as he ate.

"You're unnervingly upbeat."

"Well, I'm going to Geneva. I'm an international jetsetter now," said Ian

Tolstoy farted with perfect comic timing.

Ian replied with a huge belch.

That night, Ian lay awake listening to Susan's breathing as she slept.

Ian's secure phone buzzed against the skirting board. It was another message from Griffin.

TARGET IDENTIFIED. GENEVA HOTEL. WAR CRIMES UNIT. COVERT ELIMINATION REQUIRED. NO SPLASH.

DETAILS TO FOLLOW. WEAPONS PROVIDED LOCALLY ON ARRIVAL. NO NEED TO BRING ANYTHING THAT MIGHT UPSET CUSTOMS. YOUR FEE 4 MILLION – HALF IN ADVANCE AS USUAL.

ALSO, DUFFY. VIENNA. POSSIBLE FOLLOW-UP. PHILATELIC COVER PROVIDES PERFECT OPPORTUNITY. WE WILL ORGANISE EVERYTHING ASAP. G.

Ian rubbed his knuckles. Malcolm Duffy. The human sweater vest with a taste for mid-century British ceramics. Head of the Staffordshire Dog Mafia. The man who'd disappeared like a fart in a thunderstorm on Ian's watch. Ian wanted to get him badly. This one was personal.

He grinned.

Stamp collecting. Who knew it could be quite so exciting?

A few days later, just before his trip to Geneva, Ian returned home from another dull day of low-grade corporate chess. He opened the front door to find the family gathered like a welcoming committee at an old people's home.

"What's wrong?" asked Ian

"It's not the dog, is it?" he continued. Worried that he couldn't see Tolstoy or hear him.

Max stepped forward, holding a smart looking, gift-wrapped box. "Here. We got you a new state of the art mobile phone. All the mod-cons, with GPS, encrypted storage, doesn't look like it came out of a Christmas cracker."

"We all chipped in," Susan added helpfully. "Just in case you get lost in Geneva or get arrested for loitering near a rare post box or something."

"You'll be able to find your way around and search for places to eat too," Susan continued. "And we can find you if you get lost."

Daisy crossed her arms. "And it has a hygiene tracker and an alarm to remind you to shower every morning. Not really, but it should," she said laughing.

Ian accepted the phone solemnly, nodding like a man receiving a medal. "Touching. Truly. Thank you."

Later that evening, under the cover of darkness, he ruthlessly dismantled the phone with clinical precision, removed its SIM, and buried the non-trackable parts under the birdbath beside a particularly surly hydrangea at the end of his garden. He then took the part of the new phone that could be tracked and threw it into the back of a builder's truck with a Bristol address written on its side. The last thing he ever wanted was to be tracked by anyone. In his line of business that sort of behaviour could lead to an untimely death! He would have to think up an excuse as to where the new phone had gone when he was in Geneva.

Tolstoy sat beside him, watching approvingly, tail slapping on the ground repeatedly.

"They mean well," Ian muttered to the dog, patting the earth flat close to the birdbath, gently raking the soft soil with his fingertips – trying to disguise his excavations as carefully as he could.

Tolstoy snorted and peed on the rose bush next to the hydrangea for good measure. He didn't want a visiting dog digging up the disassembled phone at a family barbecue sometime in the future.

"Good lad," Ian said. "No sign – keep things nice and natural, that's the way."

Tolstoy slapped his tail once on the lawn in agreement.

The next morning, Ian rose at the ungodly hour of 5:17 a.m. so he could get to the airport in time for his flight. Tolstoy lifted his head, gave a sigh of such soul-deep resignation that it could have been composed by Mahler, and then flopped back down without even pretending to care. Outside, the pre-dawn street hummed with the distant grumble of milk floats, bin lorries, and foxes arguing over last night's discarded kebab.

Ian hauled himself into his grubby clothes and walked Tolstoy quickly around the block. "Keep an eye on them all while I am away," he instructed the dog. "scare burglars, kill assassins, give them no quarter boy." Tolstoy slapped his huge tail once to confirm he fully understood.

Ian quickly ate breakfast and jumped into a black cab ordered by the travel department at the Post Office. Ian dozed off in the back and before he knew it, he was almost approaching Heathrow Terminal 5, feeling stuck somewhere between drunk and hungover. He took a swig from his favourite hipflask – the dented one with a thistle emblem engraved on the front.

The black cab dropped Ian of at the departures gate with the solemnity of a hearse delivering its final payload. The driver, having endured a 10-minute monologue on the merits of curry for breakfast, simply nodded and sped away without even waiting for a tip. Ian, suitcase in one hand, a half-eaten Scotch egg in the other, limped through the automatic doors like a badly dressed diplomat from a rogue state.

Ian checked in with the minimum of fuss – his Post Office cover was water-tight and, thanks to Griffin's admin team, his boarding pass had "Post Office Philatelic Delegate" stamped on it in red. Ian liked that. Made him sound like he had gravitas. That, or a victim of an unfortunate skin condition.

He glided through security with the grace of a man who knew how to hide a blade inside the peak of a hat or the lapel of his grubby jacket. His shoes raised eyebrows, his trousers set off the explosives trace machine, but his charm – or what passed for it – disarmed everyone. Mostly because they couldn't believe a man that inept, shambolic and scruffy could ever possibly pose a serious threat to anyone.

Soon enough, Ian was reclining in the polished sterility of the Heathrow Club Lounge – a world of chrome coffee machines, hushed businessmen, and tiny croissants that tasted like crunched up cardboard.

He poured himself a glass of mid-range champagne (two-thirds of a flute, purely for stealth), and began wolfing down a tiny plate of charcuterie with the tactical precision of a soldier trained to eat on the move. He'd just loaded a second sausage roll onto his plate - and had been trying to dislodge a bit of brie from his molars with a cocktail stick - when a familiar voice sounded over his left shoulder.

"Well, look who's mingling with the frequent flyers."

Ian turned.

It was Jim.

Same old Jim. Former Royal Marine turned MI5 operative. Built like an upright freezer with a jaw you could iron shirts on. Today, he wore chinos, a blue shirt, and a lightweight windbreaker that screamed 'Dad on a mission.' His face was halfway between amusement and suspicion.

Ian blinked. "You? Are you on the mission too?"

Jim raised a paper coffee cup. "How do you know I'm not here with the wife and kids, heading for the Costa del Sol?"

"Because I saw you fake scan a boarding pass and threaten the check-in kiosk with a glare. Also, you hate Spain. Too warm. Not enough puddings."

He told Ian he was coming along as support disguised as a tired geography teacher with a passion for collecting stamps. Whether that was going to actually convince anyone was hard to say but that was the plan.

Jim smirked and pulled up a chair. "You've been briefed, then?"

Ian nodded, munching something that claimed to be a mini quiche. "Geneva. War criminal. Kosovo-scented. Very hush hush."

Jim leaned in. "Nasty bastard. Been on the radar since the Hague blew a gasket. Switzerland won't touch him – neutrality and tax shelters – so we're going to stamp him out."

"First class delivery?" Ian asked jokingly.

"Special edition. One-off. No return address," Jim answered smiling, continuing the stream of ridiculous postal related puns.

They clinked coffee cup and champagne flute in solemn camaraderie.

"Seriously though," Ian said, lowering his voice, "what are you doing on this job? I thought you didn't do field work anymore."

Jim shrugged. "They asked for subtlety. Then remembered who was on the team. So I got roped in. Besides -" he leaned back, stretching -"I've been dying for an excuse to rough up a stamp collector or two."

Ian smiled. "Well. Pack your philatelic gloves. This one's for King and country."

And with that, the two unlikely agents of chaos and retribution sat side by side in the Club Lounge, surrounded by businessmen completely oblivious to the fact that two of Britain's most dangerous men were currently arguing over who got the last miniature Danish.

Somewhere across the lounge, a toddler screamed. An espresso machine hissed. And several young lads were already drinking pints of lager at an airport bar before departing for a week of chaos in Benidorm.

And Ian, licking icing off his thumb, checked his faithful Casio watch.

It was nearly time to fly.

As they boarded the plane, Ian glanced back at the terminal. A seagull perched on the sign above the gantry opposite stared at him with those dead eyes that only birds and assassins have.

"Birds," Ian muttered. "Always bloody watching me."

And with that, he and Jim stepped aboard. Destination: Geneva.

Chapter Two
The Geneva Convention

"Some missions require a forged passport. Others require a shovel."
~ Unofficial Mossad Field Handbook, Marginalia (Possibly sarcasm)

Chapter 2
The Geneva Convention

The hotel was a vision of decadent neutrality. Perched on the edge of Lake Geneva, the Grand Helvetia Hotel looked like the kind of place where secret peace treaties were signed over truffled scrambled eggs. Crystal chandeliers sparkled with weaponised opulence, and the lobby smelt of money, polish, and very faintly of goose.

Ian Taylor stepped through the revolving doors with all the confidence of a man who had just brushed naan breadcrumbs from his underpants in the taxi from the airport. He wore a linen blazer two decades too young for him and a cravat he'd found in his penthouse apartment's emergency disguise drawer. He gave his name at reception, received his keycard, and was swiftly ushered up to the third floor by a concierge who looked like he judged people as a professional sport.

"Welcome to the Grand Helvetia Hotel," the man intoned.

"And to you, my good man," Ian replied with theatrical grandeur, before tripping slightly over his own wheelie suitcase and farting audibly. The lift doors closed. The lift now smelling slightly of eggy fart with a hint of cheap Whisky.

His room was tastefully beige, in the sort of way that screamed money and repressed personality. A huge bed dominated the centre, dressed with more cushions than a medieval throne room. Ian admired the minibar with the reverence of a monk approaching a Buddhist shrine. Then he opened his case, changed into a pair of old, worn, frayed jeans, a stripy t-shirt with questionable elasticity, and trainers that looked like they'd been rescued from a garbage tip.

He was meeting Jim for a few drinks and some dinner. They also need to plan.

By 7:30pm, they were seated outside a lakeside bistro called Les Fous Fromage, which roughly translated to The Cheese Crazies. Ian had chosen it purely because the menu had an entire page dedicated to melted cheesy things.

The view was postcard perfect. Lake Geneva shimmered like a vat of mineral water designed by God. Swans glided about like pompous waiters in long white suits. And the Alps loomed in the distance with a brooding menace that reminded Ian of Ruth in the monthly performance team meeting back in London.

Jim looked relaxed, in his own fashion – which still involved being alert enough to kill a man with a dessert spoon if provoked. He was drinking a local beer. Ian was already on his second carafe of wine and deeply invested in a fondue.

"Do you trust that all that cheese?" Jim asked, eyeing the hot bubbling pot.

"Absolutely not," Ian said, skewering a cube of bread and dipping it into the volcanic hot cheese. "But that's part of the thrill."

They ate heartily. Between mouthfuls of raclette and suspicious cured meats, they shared past tales of bureaucratic idiocy and previous assignments that had ended in disaster, success, diplomatic immunity, and – in one case – the accidental poisoning of a minor member of an obscure European royal family.

Eventually, as the stars began to twinkle and Ian attempted to order a third crème brûlée, Jim handed him a small, slim, highly secure, velvet-lined case.

"Special issue," Jim said quietly. "Limited edition stamp. Unusual colour. A collector would love to own it. Ink laced with Class V neurotoxin. Slow acting. Goes through the mucous membranes. Lick it, send it, done. He dies 'naturally; in his sleep 4 – 6 hours later. No fuss, no mess."

Ian took it reverently.

"But will he actually want to post it?" asked Ian.

"Yes, apparently the stamp is more valuable with a postal stamp marking if you are a collector. You can offer to hand stamp it for him and there's a special celebratory envelope, or 'cover', as these stamp collecting fanatics call them. Apparently, all these things make the stamp even more valuable," said Jim shrugging.

"Beats me," concurred Ian.

"Don't touch the back of the stamp with your bare hands. Best you wear gloves when you handle it – or just let him take it from the case." Jim concluded.

"Post Office would be proud," he said, sliding the secure case into his inner jacket pocket.

Jim nodded. "Whatever you do don't get it mixed up with your souvenir postcards and send it to Susan and your kids back home."

Ian laughed, "Indeed!"

They wandered along the promenade after dinner, Ian clutching a takeaway espresso the size of a thimble, Jim scanning the shadows as naturally as other men check football scores on a Saturday afternoon.

"So, you're at the Helvetia," Jim said, flicking a cigarette butt into the lake with sniper-like precision. "I'm at the Hotel Pension Edelweiss. No minibar, no irony, one angry goat outside my window."

"Them's the breaks! You can spend the day in my room tomorrow on guard duty if you like," Ian said. "And I never trust hotels without irony."

Jim shrugged. "I can sleep in your room for some of tomorrow. My job is to keep an eye on the outside tonight. I've also hacked into your hotel's CCTV, it's like looking inside a Bond villain's lair – I can see everywhere. I'll be watching you and the rest of the hotel. You prep for tomorrow. Get a good night's sleep. And charm the stamp collecting nutcases tomorrow – before moving in on our Kosovan war criminal before bedtime."

The Headhunter

Jim and Ian parted with a huge celebratory whoop and a fist bump. This made two passing teenage tourists laugh. They thought the big shambling, scruffy man and his tough looking friend seemed a bit out of place in this millionaires' playground.

"Don't do anything I wouldn't do, sweet cheeks," Jim called.

"Then I'm allowed three fondue-related injuries and a diplomatic incident involving a spa," Ian replied.

Jim laughed, then disappeared into the Geneva night like a man born to melt like piping hot cheese.

Back in his hotel room, Ian placed the poisoned stamp, secure in its protective case, carefully in a drawer beside the Gideon Bible and a novelty sewing kit. Then he opened his laptop, began drafting a few pithy phrases for his panel speech the next day about "Collecting Se-tenant Strips," and fell asleep halfway through typing the word "perforations."

Lake Geneva glittered in the moonlight. Somewhere not far away, a war criminal finished his last cigar, oblivious to the dark, postal harbinger of death that awaited him the next day.

That night Ian Taylor dreamed of eagles, old stamps featuring sea horses, and Fondue moitié-moitié truffée à la royale – garnished with white Alba truffle shavings and a whisper of 24k gold leaf, served with gold-dusted croutons, a side of wagyu charcuterie and small glass of 1960s vintage Fendant – chilled to perfection.

Mind you, the dream eventually took a nasty turn. Ian ended up seated on the lakeside terrace of *Le Fromage*

Éternel – Geneva's most exclusive fondue restaurant, where the fondue is served in hand-thrown ceramic pots by waiters in starched white gloves. Much to the dismay of nearby oligarchs Ian in his dream pulled out a battered Greggs sausage roll from his jacket pocket – declaring loudly "emergency rations" - and then dunked it directly into the bubbling royal fondue pot with a triumphant *plop*, splashing truffle oil onto the waiter's trousers.

After a fitful night caused by far too much fondue both real and dreamt Ian hauled himself out of his giant bed and got ready for what would be a busy day – with him on his feet for most of it. He wondered what was for breakfast – he was starving.

His stomach gurgled ominously as he staggered upright, belched once, farted twice and made for the bathroom with the urgency of a man trying to beat a ticking clock.

He showered briskly, shaved with a hotel razor that removed two moles and most of his upper lip, and applied deodorant with the solemnity of a priest anointing the dying. Then, he waddled toward the lift, buttoning his shirt over a belly that looked like it had been inflated on purpose, humming "God Save the King" and thinking about sausages.

The Grand Helvetia's breakfast buffet was held in a huge room that looked like the inside of a Fabergé egg. Chandeliers twinkled above like icebergs suspended in space. Crisp white linen covered tables with more forks than one man should ever be expected to understand. The staff floated about in tailcoats and solemnity, and a string quartet in the corner played something so tasteful and refined it almost made Ian cry.

And then he saw it.

The buffet.

It stretched the entire length of the huge room. Gleaming. Endless. A living altar to cholesterol, excess, raised sugar levels and culinary diplomacy. The Swiss knew how to do neutrality, but they were also very, very good at breakfast.

Ian was in his element.

There were trays of golden rösti, glistening like treasure. Platters of cured meats: Black Forest ham, Bündnerfleisch, mortadella, all fanned out like edible luxury carpeting. Cheeses galore – Emmental, Gruyère, Appenzeller, each with its own little flag, as if proud of their nationhood. There were eggs in every conceivable format: scrambled, poached, boiled, devilled, Benedict-ed. An omelette station run by a man who looked like he had once cooked for dictators. Bowls of muesli that looked like small gravel pits and pots of yoghurt so organic they were probably still mooing.

Then came the breads: crusty sourdough, croissants big enough to sleep in, glossy brioches, dark rye with seeds like shrapnel. A waffle station with six kinds of syrups and whipped cream that defied gravity. Bowls of jewel-like fruit, compotes, clotted creams, pastries, tiny Danish things that screamed *wealth* in twelve languages.

There was even a section labelled "English Breakfast", which Ian surveyed with a raised eyebrow. Sausages, bacon, beans, black pudding. Respectable. But they'd put the baked beans in very tiny silver urns. *Cowards.*

He was seated at a table by a woman in black who looked like she'd been trained by Interpol to monitor jam theft. Ian nodded politely, adjusted his napkin, then launched himself at the buffet like a man emerging from a six-year fast.

What followed was an act of culinary carnage that would later be referred to by the hotel staff as *The Incident.*

He began with the English section. Two sausages (one pork, one 'mystery'), bacon folded into a waffle station waffle, four small urns of beans poured together so aggressively the tomato sauce sloshed onto the tablecloth, and an entire fried egg sandwich he constructed himself using brioche buns and Emmental. He turned to the cheese section like a Roman emperor spotting Gaul on a map. He scooped up slices of Gruyère with his bare hands, pairing them with walnuts and stuffing it into his mouth with the fervour of a man escaping capture.

He moved along the buffet like a scavenging bear, loading his plate with smoked salmon, anchovies (because why not?), and a dollop of jam from the 'local preserve' stand that was clearly meant to be shared. He dropped a huge croissant into his jacket pocket "for later" and used a flat bread as a napkin.

"Sir," said a young waiter nervously as Ian began ladling clotted cream onto a waffle already topped with cheese and jam, "that is meant to be separate from the savoury items."

Ian blinked at him. "Life is about contrast, Pierre," he said solemnly, reading the young waiter's name badge. "Ever tried cheddar with marmalade? It'll change your life forever."

He returned to the table with a plate so piled it looked like a large Henry Moore bronze of sin and temptation in the grounds of a State Museum. As he approached, the string quartet faltered briefly – possibly out of fear of what might happen if Ian tripped – his plate was piled so high.

He sat. He ate. He grunted like a contented sow.

At one point, he pulled the croissant from his pocket, broke it open, and inserted a small sausage and some mustard. He dubbed it a *Helvetic Hot Dog* and made a note to trademark it later.

Midway through a fourth pastry, Jim appeared at the table, holding a coffee and wearing a face of quiet horror.

"Jesus Christ," he said, "are you *catering* the assassination?"

Ian looked up, mouth now full of pickled herring. "Energy," he said, spraying a small slick of fennel-scented olive oil spittle across the fine white linen. "I'm getting my strength up."

"You're a disgrace," Jim muttered, sipping his black coffee. "A beautiful, unholy disgrace."

"Thank you," Ian beamed, and dunked the last of his sausage croissant into a ramekin of maple syrup. Breakfast had well and truly been served.

And then to work.

The Geneva Stamp & Philatelic International Collectibles Expo was being held in the hotel's grand ballroom. The room was a riot of velvet ropes, display cases, and the quiet hum of obsessive men comparing gum residue, perforations and the precise colour of each stamp.

Ian surveyed the crowd.

There were wealthy eccentrics in crumpled linen, a smattering of retired colonels with improbable moustaches, and a surprisingly high number of women named Ingrid. Stamps in rare mint condition exchanged hands like fine miniature works of art. Overhead, music played – something baroque.

Jim loitered nearby. He wore a badge that read "Peter Gilbert – Geography teacher – Collector of Machins," and chewed noisily on a cinnamon toothpick. Ian gave him a nod. It was time to get down to business.

The target appeared at 11:04 a.m. precisely. He was tall, silver-haired, and polished like a high-end coffin. His accent still carried the hard edges of the Balkans, though his passport now said Argentine and he claimed to have lived in Patagonia since the early 2000s. He wore a cream linen suit and a small felt hat, the kind that suggested both privilege and delusion.

His real name was Miloš Draganovic, but on the conference programme he was listed as "Dr Milan D. Rados, Honorary Fellow of the Patagonian Philatelic Society." His official biography noted a long-standing fascination with South American commemorative issues and "regional postal routes in post-conflict economies." There was no mention, of course, of his years as a senior commander in the Yugoslav Army during the Kosovo conflict, nor of the war crimes tribunal that had tried – and failed – to bring him to The Hague.

Ian spotted him at the Uruguay booth, where Miloš was squinting at a 1924 five-centavo with all the intensity of a man reliving past sins. His hands were manicured, his gaze laser-focused, and his aura reeked of money, fear, and a lifetime of secrets swept under extremely expensive rugs.

Ian approached him at the Uruguay booth, where Dr. Milan was squinting at a 1924 five-centavo with lust.

"Rare overprint," Ian said, leaning in. "But the gum's suspect. Too much gloss."

Dr. Milan turned, eyebrows raised. "You collect South American issues?"

"I dabble. I know someone who might be able to get you the 1933 Tierra del Fuego set. Mint condition. If you are interested."

Dr. Milan's eyes gleamed.

"Yes, I would be very interested."

"What are you doing for dinner tonight?" Milan asked.

"Tonight, 8pm. In the rooftop restaurant here in the hotel?" Ian replied. "I'll see if I can persuade the seller to let me bring them with me."

"I'd be willing to pay well if they are mint," Dr Milan continued.

The rest of the day seemed something of an anticlimax for Ian. He continued talking to a host of stamp fanatics, but he couldn't stop thinking about his task later that evening.

He hid frequently throughout the day behind the shell of the event stand swigging at his hip flask of Scotch – purely for medicinal reasons, of course.

They met that evening in the hotel's rooftop restaurant. Candlelight. Foie gras. Waiters that floated. Dr. Milan spoke at length about stamps, thermodynamics, and the inherent flaws of the Schengen Agreement. Ian nodded, laughed, and slid a beautifully made leather presentation case across the table. Inside a full mint 1933 Tierra del Fuego set.

"I can arrange for them to be released to you tomorrow if you are interested." Said Ian.

Dr. Milan looked in awe and said, "Oh yes, I am very interested indeed.

"I'll introduce you to the owner tomorrow morning and the pair of you can agree a suitable price that suits you both," Ian teased.

"Can't you sell them to me now," said Dr. Milan frantic to buy them.

"Sadly not, but I am assured the owner is keen to sell. I am sure you will be able to come to a suitable arrangement," said Ian.

"While we are about it," Ian continued, "you might be interested in this too."

"These just came in from London this afternoon. Pre-issue proofs of the £1 Sea Horse reprints. Royal Mail only ever printed thirty sets in Tyrian Plum before they changed the plates. I can let you have one if you are interested. I'm only giving them to a few very special individuals."

Dr. Milan opened the secure case Ian had pushed gently across the table and let out a soft groan of pleasure. He delicately fingered the stamp like a man revisiting an old lover. Ian then produced a specially produced envelope – with details of the event beautifully printed on the front.

"Add it to this special event cover – only 100 in existence – and mail it to yourself in Argentina. A unique postal mark will increase the value considerably too. Here, I have a special event themed hand stamp I can use now if that helps."

Dr. Milan nodded enthusiastically. He moistened the stamp with his small darting lizard like tongue and then pressed the stamp gently but firmly onto the special envelope.

Ian then very carefully hand stamped it and handed it to the waiter for posting.

"Thank you so much," said Dr. Milan excitedly. "Dinner is definitely on me tonight."

Ian sipped his Armagnac and watched the moment pass. The adhesive had been treated with a compound developed in the MI5 laboratory. Slow release. Metabolised. Undetectable.

Dr Milan D. Rados would die in his sleep that night. He would leave behind only stamps, silence, and a very startled maid.

The next morning, Ian went down to breakfast full of anticipation. Not because he wanted to confirm whether Dr Milan D. Rados – Honorary Fellow of the Patagonian Philatelic Society and genocidal former commander of the Drina Wolves Brigade – had expired peacefully in his sleep with a poison that leaves no trace. No. That, Ian assumed, had gone precisely to plan. The real excitement – the true fulfilment – lay in once again throwing himself face-first into the Grand Helvetia Hotel's legendary breakfast buffet.

In he strode, much to the alarm of the small army of waiters. They recognised him instantly – the British delegate who'd made headlines across the hotel's internal WhatsApp group the day before by eating five separate breakfasts, spilling cappuccino into a piano, and burping loudly enough to make the Swiss ambassador to Sweden choke on his compote.

Ian arrived in a waft of shampoo and vintage Brut aftershave. He wore the same food-flecked clothes from the night before, now also dappled with mysterious fondue-based stains, and a pair of trousers that had seen better centuries. His gait was purposeful. His stomach was growling. His bowels already threatening rebellion.

"Bon matin," said a small, impeccably dressed maître d', attempting polite restraint.

"Absolutely," Ian replied, belching loudly, nodding at nothing in particular, and steaming past the maître d' toward the buffet like an Orca in a feeding frenzy.

The spread was once again a thing of legend: towers of cured meats, battalions of cheeses arranged by altitude and smell, baskets of viennoiserie so golden they could have been spun from Rapunzel's hair, trays of eggs done five different ways, slow-roasted tomatoes with garlic and thyme, hash browns like golden paving slabs, twelve types of granola, today three live omelette stations, and – curiously – a chocolate fountain positioned between the gluten-free bread and an enormous jug of bircher muesli.

Ian got to work.

He started with five sausages. Three were pork, one was allegedly veal, and one had some sort of local liqueur in it. He balanced them on top of an enormous slab of rösti, added a fried duck egg for flair, and garnished the plate with six strips of bacon and a half wedge of baked camembert "just to round things out."

"Full Swiss," he muttered with glee, loading it up with a ladle of onion gravy from the 'traditional toppings' urn.

On his second trip to the food stations, he returned with a bowl the size of a motorcyclist's helmet, filled with bircher muesli, four spoons of Nutella, a dollop of crème fraîche, and what looked like crushed hazelnut brittle. As he passed the croissants, he grabbed two – one under each arm like a man smuggling edible boomerangs. They would, he reasoned, make excellent napkins if nothing else.

He washed it all down with two espressos, three glasses of orange juice, a lukewarm mimosa left on a neighbouring table by an Instagram influencer with digestive issues, and a large mug of builder's tea he'd made himself using six tea bags and a kettle he'd found in a cupboard under one of the omelette stations.

The waiters looked on in stunned silence, as if watching a hippo dismantle an allotment.

At one point, Ian leaned back to stretch and let loose a belch so seismic it rattled the cutlery on the table of a startled Scandinavian couple beside him.

"Pardon," he said with exaggerated formality, before letting out another, softer echo-burp that seemed to make the maître d' physically wilt.

A small child – perhaps seven – wandered over to marvel at Ian's fourth plate of food. Ian looked down at her, then theatrically placed a single boiled egg into his mouth whole. He cracked the shell open with his teeth like a walnut and winked. She ran back crying loudly to her mother, who was already shielding her eyes with a linen napkin.

Undeterred, Ian moved on to the sweet table. Two waffles. A crêpe. A cinnamon roll. A pain au chocolat. A slice of Sachertorte ("Technically Austrian but spiritually breakfast," he declared). Then – as if some long-forgotten sense of balance awoke within him – a single raspberry.

"Mustn't forget the healthy option," Ian pronounced loudly to anyone who might be listening.

By now, his stomach was beginning to groan in protest, but Ian paid it no heed. He stood, patted his belly, and released a fart of such stealthy malevolence it caused the sommelier arranging glassware by the juice station to double over silently dropping two glasses onto the floor, shards of glass flying everywhere.

The man next to Ian at the coffee machine looked over and whispered in broken English, "You... very strong man."

Ian nodded gravely. "One does what one must."

Having eaten somewhere in the region of six thousand calories and what one guest later described as "the hopes and dreams of three nations," Ian finally pushed back from his table and ambled toward the lifts, belching steadily like a foghorn running out of fuel.

He gave the maître d' a jaunty salute.

"Same time tomorrow?" he said.

The maître d' did not respond. He simply stared into the middle distance, muttering something about needing a new job. Or possibly a programme of psychotherapy sessions.

And with that, Ian disappeared back upstairs, already loosening his belt and wondering what might be on offer in the hall later. Perhaps just a little cheese. And maybe something sweet. Something small. A palate cleanser. A petit four. Or twelve.

Geneva had been good to him so far.

And the day had only just begun.

Back at the event later that morning, Ian browsed a nearby booth, with Jim at his side, dedicated to Scandinavian semi-postals while chewing a muesli bar with alarming ferocity.

At a little after 11am the Police had arrived at the hotel, then an ambulance, then a black undertaker's van. Ian watched quietly as what he could only imagine was the body of Dr Milan D. Rados was discretely removed and transported away. Off to the morgue for a cut and dried confirmation of 'died of natural causes' by the local coroner.

"What you reap, you must sow", announced Ian loudly to Jim and everyone else standing near them both.

Then across the hall, he noticed something.

A man.

Hatchet-faced. Thin lips. Impossibly well-ironed shirt. Standing too still. Far too still.

He wasn't browsing. He wasn't even pretending to browse. He was *watching* Ian – the way a hawk might watch a small mammal just before a dive. Cold-eyed. Deliberate. He had the kind of presence that made you instinctively tighten your belt and check your life insurance.

Ian shifted slightly to the left behind a Belgian colonial stamp display and pretended to read a plaque about Congo overprints. Then he looked again.

Still there. The man hadn't moved a millimetre. Except now... he was smiling. A thin, mirthless smile that suggested he had recently poisoned the entire population of a medium sized village and rather enjoyed it.

Ian whispered sideways to Jim, who was pretending to browse a case of rare Icelandic fish stamps with all the interest of a bored customs officer.

"Jim. One for you to tail. Hatchet-faced. Section B, next to the Norwegians. Looks like he irons his soul."

Jim didn't even blink. "Got him," he said, eyes casually shifting with the grace of a seasoned predator.

The man turned and began strolling along the outer edge of the exhibits. Jim moved in parallel, always one row behind, flicking through an overpriced collection of Liechtenstein railway issue stamps on the way, with a look of vague distaste.

Fifteen minutes later, Hatchet Face made his exit – through a side door labelled "Delegates Only," which, naturally, no one ever enforced. He didn't look back.

Ian remained in the hall, flipping through Mongolian commemoratives, pausing at a curious first-day cover featuring puffins in ceremonial dress. He made a show of interest, asking the vendor of the stall if the birds had names.

Meanwhile, Jim followed Hatchet Face.

Outside, the midday Geneva sun bounced off the cobbled streets and cast long shadows from the baroque lampposts. Hatchet Face walked briskly, with the clipped precision of a man used to counting steps and escape routes. He didn't check his phone. He didn't check a map. He *knew* exactly where he was going.

Jim kept a casual distance, stopping occasionally to inspect a window display or scratch his shin. He passed a group of university students arguing over fondue, a cyclist singing opera along with his AirPods, and an elderly woman who stared at Jim with unsettling familiarity. He tipped an imaginary hat.

Hatchet Face walked down into the old town, taking a turn past a cathedral where a busker was playing Radiohead on a cello. Then another turn, down a side street of antique shops and shuttered galleries. Finally, the man ducked into a small café that seemed to serve nothing but baguettes and cheese.

Jim didn't follow him in.

Instead, he perched at a wine bar across the square, ordered a glass of local white, and waited. Surveillance, he believed, should always include decent seating and the potential for fine food and wine.

Twenty-three minutes later, Hatchet Face emerged carrying a paper-wrapped baguette and a cup of coffee so small it could only legally be classed as a suggestion. He walked with no urgency, but with purpose – down two more streets, across a quiet roundabout, and into the pine-stitched edges of a suburb that looked like it had been designed by someone nostalgic for 1982.

He entered a small village square. There was a fountain. A post box. A woman yelling at her schnauzer in rapid Swiss-German. Hatchet Face crossed the square and disappeared into a flower shop under a pink awning that said *Fleurs de Joie* in a delicate, looping gold font.

Jim waited. Then circled the block. He passed a bakery – the smell of butter and yeast temporarily disarming – and hoisted himself onto a steel bin with a quiet grunt. It groaned under his weight but held. From this makeshift perch, he could just see into the narrow back alley that ran behind the flower shop.

The door creaked open.

Out stepped the Bear Man. Jim and Ian had history with the Bear Man.

Bigger than Jim remembered. Maybe it was the apron – grey, dusted with pollen, stretched across a barrel chest like a butcher dressing as a florist for a community play. His beard was more sculpted now, but his eyes were still piggy and alert.

He carried a crate of peonies with all the delicacy of a man hauling a corpse. Jim reached slowly for his phone and snapped two photos. He blinked, trying to process the next figure stepping through the door.

Behind him – smiling faintly, just like he had in every one of Ian's cursed memories – was Malcolm Duffy, Ian's nemesis.

Not in a disguise. Not trying to hide. Just… there. Wearing a tasteful cashmere scarf a very boring cardigan, monogrammed slippers and a smug expression. The man who'd vanished. Who'd outfoxed MI5 surveillance. Who'd once shown Ian a rhododendron with tears in his eyes.

Duffy reached out, patted the Bear Man on the shoulder, and nodded toward the far end of the alley. The Bear Man lumbered off and loaded the peonies into the back of a nondescript Volvo estate that was parked nearby.

Duffy walked slowly behind and got into the back of the car like a man who'd never once in his life ordered the deaths of several policemen in Albania or the children of a Russian defector. Hatchet Face climbed into the car next to Duffy.

Then Jim watched as they drove off - taking pictures of the car and its number plate.

Jim stayed frozen. The bin groaned again.

Back at the hotel, Ian was biting into a commemorative biscuit shaped like the Swiss canton of Vaud. His phone buzzed.

Photo. *Duffy. Clear as day.*

Text: *"The Bear is back. So is Duffy."*

Ian blinked. Then whispered aloud to no one in particular, "Oh bloody hell. Why is he always one step ahead?"

The bloody puffins could wait Ian concluded.

Ian watched a documentary about penguin migration and pretended to be a man who hadn't just assassinated a war criminal using a highly poisonous rare stamp.

Ian smiled.

Nothing bloomed in Geneva quite like revenge.

It was almost time to fly home to a loving but nagging wife, two recalcitrant kids and an ever loyal, unfeasibly large dog.

But there was just one last buffet breakfast to tackle.

To the victor go the spoils of war...

Chapter Three
Vienna Waltz

"Revenge is best served cold. Preferably during brunch."
~ Unattributed, but widely quoted in GCHQ canteen graffiti (now removed)

Chapter 3

Vienna Waltz

Ian Taylor arrived back in London with the look of a man who had been force-fed 6,000 calories for breakfast every day and then another 6,000 for dinner. Which, of course, he had – though "force-fed" implied resistance, and there had been none. He had welcomed every melted cheese, spiced sausage, schnitzel-soaked moment with open arms and a gaping mouth. His body now resembled a one-man tribute to the Zeppelin.

He emerged from the arrivals gate at Heathrow dragging a suitcase that rattled and squealed ominously with each step, like it might be carrying a disgruntled family of marmots. He returned with emotional baggage, literal baggage, and a suspiciously clinking duty-free bag labelled *"Alpen Power – 60% ABV for Real Men."*

Outside, he climbed into the back of a black cab and nestled into the seat like an overfed grizzly bear preparing for hibernation. Within 90 seconds, he was sleeping so soundly the driver checked the rearview mirror twice to confirm he was still alive.

When the cab finally wheezed to a halt outside his home in North London, Ian unfolded himself from the back seat, paid the driver with a mixture of UK Sterling, crumpled Euros, a Werther's Original and a very old 10 Franc note, and waddled off towards his front door.

Susan met him with the expression of a woman who had spent a week trying to make peace with the universe and then found it had come home early and needed a shower.

"You smell of cheese, Daddy," she said, arms crossed, screwing her nose up.

"Swiss efficiency, Mummy," Ian replied, attempting a suave forehead kiss that missed and landed somewhere near her left ear. "And possibly some trout fondue. Don't ask."

He handed her a box of expensive chocolates with the flourish of a man giving the crown jewels to a woman who really just wanted him to put the bins out. Then he produced a bottle of violent green schnapps labelled *Waldgeist: Der Kieferbrenner*. The label featured a woodcut of a gleeful forest goblin vomiting into a cauldron surrounded by medicinal herbs and what might have been a flaming log.

"I thought it might help with your chakras," Ian offered helpfully.

Susan squinted at it. "It looks like it could clean an oven."

"I think that it probably already has," Ian nodded, pleased.

At that moment, Max appeared in the hallway, eyeing his father like a bomb disposal expert sizing up a suspicious package.

"Is that your actual suitcase?"

Ian looked down at the lumpy excuse for a suitcase on wheels. It had been duct-taped shut in three places, bulged at unnatural angles, and one wheel squeaked like a traumatised gerbil playing a tiny violin.

"It's a classic," he said proudly. "Like me. A little broken. A little noisy. Smells of herring."

Max said nothing, but the sigh he emitted carried the weight of seven generations of disappointed sons.

Daisy appeared via FaceTime on an iPad propped against a bowl of fruit. Susan had clearly been mid-sentence with her when Ian had arrived home. Her face was sun-drenched and pixelated, the background all tropical trees and howling monkeys. She was now out in Belize – working remotely.

"Tell me," she said flatly, "that you didn't come back with another bloody snow globe."

Ian grinned and, like a magician, produced it from his inner coat pocket. "Ta-da!"

Inside, a tiny model of the *Hotel Grand Helvetia* stood perched atop a mirrored base. When shaken, it snowed tiny chocolate flakes and something that looked suspiciously like glittering parmesan.

Daisy stared. "So predictable. You're like a walking episode of *Junk in the Attic: Trauma Edition*."

Susan took the globe, gave it a single unimpressed shake, and watched the flakes fall with an air of mild disdain.

"You're not putting that on the mantelpiece," she said.

"Too late," Ian replied, already heading for the living room. "It's going next to the Himalayan yak bell and the limited edition commemorative Toblerone from Geneva airport last time I was there. I'm creating a vibe."

"You're creating a museum of poor decisions," muttered Max.

"I call it a shrine to international diplomacy," Ian countered, flopping onto the sofa with the grace of a falling tree.

Susan sniffed the air. "What else is in that suitcase?"

"Mostly laundry. And… a bag of cured sausages. Don't worry, only mildly radioactive by now."

"Did you actually *do* any work while you were there?" Daisy asked, squinting suspiciously.

"Absolutely," Ian said firmly. "I stamped things. Shook hands. And I ate huge amounts of delicious food. Oh, and I had a massage. All in a day's work."

Susan rolled her eyes. "And you're not planning on unpacking until…?"

"I thought I'd give it a week. Let it acclimatise. Like a fine cheese."

"Like an actual health hazard," replied Susan, already at her wits end with Ian. And he had only been back home 10 minutes.

Ian smiled, sipped some of the mystery schnapps he had brought back from a tea mug, and let out a satisfied belch.

He was home.

Tolstoy barked once and farted twice – overcome with joy that his lord and master had finally returned from international gluttony and mild bouts of espionage.

"He's missed you terribly, Daddy," said Susan, stepping smartly aside before the dog's excitement caused further atmospheric disruption.

"I've missed him too Mummy...and I missed you," he said turning looking at Susan with an affectionate smile.

"I missed you too Daddy."

Ian settled back into the rhythm of normal domestic life – comforting and reassuring, less calories, less danger.

After a few weeks back in London though – a blur of continual unsolicited advice from Susan, precisely-timed nagging, and breakfasts so aggressively wholesome they seemed designed to erase all joy – Ian Taylor was restless again. The granola had no sugar. The tea was herbal. And Ian needed someone or something to get his teeth into.

At work. Ruth continued insist on regular 'catch ups' and 'one-to-ones', which frankly drove Ian quietly insane. He despised the endless box ticking and process of corporate life.

Tolstoy had developed a theatrical limp Ian strongly suspected was pure acting. Every time someone mentioned the word "walk," the dog would produce the limp with the tragic flair of an Oscar nominee.

"You are just a bloody liar Tolstoy, stop making things up," Ian bellowed at Tolstoy. But it just made the dog worse.

Ian needed out. Mentally, emotionally, digestively.

Fortunately help was only just around the corner in the shape of the next event on Ian's philatelic calendar – a black-tie event in Vienna.

Not for schnitzel. Not for sachertorte. Not even for the delightfully punctual trams. No – he was chasing a ghost in brogues. Mr Malcolm Duffy. Slippery, smug, and with a wardrobe that suggested that he had always lived very close to a local charity shop.

Duffy had risen – or rather, slithered – into the role of Ian's personal tormentor. A cardiganed phantom. And Ian was in no mood for reconciliation.

To the casual observer, Duffy seemed harmless: a slightly clammy, middle-aged man with a fondness for knitwear and Staffordshire dog figurines. But beneath that fusty exterior lurked a man with a taste for sabotage, subterfuge, and (if MI5 reports were accurate) the sort of body count usually reserved for small civil wars.

He'd disappeared from London without a trace, save for one suspicious porcelain spaniel – booby-trapped and left in a north London living room like a gift from Satan's Etsy store. Mercifully, it hadn't gone off.

Then came Geneva. Ian and Jim had spotted Hatchet Face skulking through a stamp expo, eyeing philatelic rarities like he was picking out venomous mushrooms. They hadn't known if Duffy was following Ian, or if Ian was following Duffy – or if it was all some mad symphony of floral arrangements, coded messages, peonies, and an enormous man with a beard like shagpile carpet and the smile of a tranquilised wolf.

Thanks to Griffin's team – and a combination of aggressive data scraping, light bribery, and one surprisingly loose-lipped Viennese florist – Duffy's trail led to Vienna.

Operating under a new alias: "Herr Alois Kerbler." Allegedly a reclusive collector of obscure postal ephemera, Nazi-era dachshund memorabilia, and other interests best not spoken aloud in civilised society.

Of course it would be Vienna, Ian thought. He hated Vienna.

The Headhunter

A city of Freud, facades, facial hair and cakes that required scaffolding. A place where the coffee had more rules than MI5, and even the pigeons judged you.

Which is how it came to pass that, on a chilly Thursday morning in late November, the dignified citizens of Vienna remained blissfully unaware that their beloved Grand Kaiserhof Hotel – a place that boasted five stars, an oyster bar, and plumbing of remarkable historical interest – was playing host to a heavily perspiring man in a tuxedo, that was far too tight, and his tough looking friend.

The hotel had a guest list that included minor royalty, major crooks, and at least three people under permanent Interpol watch. The carpet was so plush it made your ankles nervous, and the chandeliers looked like they'd been stolen directly from the Habsburg treasury.

Ian Taylor – rogue Post Office worker, freelance assassin, and part-time editor of the Stamp Collector's Bulletin – was currently wedging himself into a crushed velvet armchair in the lobby with the grim commitment of a man who knew his trousers didn't fit when he packed them, and they sure as hell didn't fit him now.

His tuxedo was too tight, his shirt had developed a button-based vendetta, and his bow tie sat at an angle that suggested it had lost the will to live sometime around Heathrow.

In one pocket: a naked Mini Babybel. In the other: the crushed remains of a packet of salt and vinegar crisps. Also, the unmistakable aroma of last night's lamb vindaloo radiated from his every pore.

The lobby, with its gold-leaf ceiling and priceless tapestries, was not prepared.

But then, neither was Vienna.

He adjusted his bowtie with the care of someone disarming a minor explosive, then removed a partly crushed crisp from his inside pocket and ate it thoughtfully.

The mission was simple. Track Duffy. Confirm location. Establish pattern. Wait for the moment...then bang! Gone!

As with most of Ian's operations, the "wait for the moment" bit would likely involve various digestive issues, at least one awkward misunderstanding involving a cultural faux pas, and probably a chase through a crowded art gallery.

But for now, Ian leaned back, crossed his legs, and began making mental notes in the only way he knew how – through caffeine, salted snacks, and some more of those delicious French fries dusted with a fine truffle powder that seemed to be doing the rounds in the hotel lobby.

Jim and Ian were due to attend a special gala tonight – a black-tie launch for the new *WWII Rare Stamps and Resistance Letters* exhibition at the Vienna National Postal Museum. It was technically part of Ian's Post Office itinerary. But unofficially, it was bait. Bait for Duffy, who couldn't resist two things: 1) rare commemorative items of imperial decline, and 2) the chance to humiliate Ian at every turn.

Unfortunately, Ian had not worn a tuxedo in well over a decade. And this one, borrowed from Griffin's trunk of disguises, had the faint smell of mothballs, cheap cologne, and something that could well be gun oil or plastic explosives. The trousers clung to Ian's thighs with the desperation of a recently jilted lover, and the bow tie looked like it had been tied by a man in a strong crosswind.

The hotel concierge, with the poise of a Viennese undertaker, had raised an eyebrow as Ian shuffled through the marble lobby earlier that evening – clearly trying to decide whether this strange Englishman was here to stay at the hotel or to rob it.

Now, stood in front of a giant gold-framed mirror near the lifts, Ian tried to straighten his cummerbund and failed.

"You look like an ageing magician from Basildon," Jim muttered, as Ian flicked a rogue crisp crumb across the hotel lobby.

Ian adjusted his waistband for the fifth time and squinted at himself in the mirror again. It didn't help.

"Very Daniel Craig," Ian said to no one in particular. "If Craig had been raised by wolves and fed exclusively on leftover chicken korma."

Somewhere beyond the ballroom doors, a string quartet began their third pass at *The Blue Danube*, and Ian inhaled deeply.

He was here in Vienna for Duffy.

He was here for revenge.

That and the seven million pounds offered by the CIA and Mossad who had suffered several lost agents at the hands of Duffy's team over the past decade.

And also, potentially, for the miniature pork schnitzel canapés rumoured to be circulating on trays in and around the hotel at any given moment.

It was late Autumn – on the run up to Christmas time.

Outside, the snow-flecked streets of Vienna gleamed with festive energy. But Ian had no time for winter markets or overpriced glühwein. There was a gala to attend – stamp related.

Jim and Ian walked quickly. Jim holding a large golfing umbrella to shield them from the weather.

The National Postal Museum was a baroque monstrosity filled with stamp cases, hushed whispers, and the kind of lighting that made everyone look like they'd died in 1892. The gala had been arranged to celebrate the unveiling of a newly discovered set of WWII-era postal proofs – some from the Eastern Front, others allegedly printed in secret in the closing days of the Third Reich.

It was a black-tie affair, thick with pretension and expensive perfume. Ian swept in, trying to look like he belonged. His entrance was only slightly marred by the fact his left shoe squeaked with every step. Still, he took a canapé, nodded gravely at a man discussing ink absorbency, and made a beeline for the nearest glass of champagne.

Jim was posing as an Eastern European philatelic correspondent. His name badge read: Ivano Rumpel – Transylvanian Stamp Weekly.

"You look like a penguin that got fired from the zoo in that suit," Ian muttered.

"And you smell like Surstromming and chutney," Jim replied, sipping his drink.

"I think you'll find that Surstromming is Swedish," said Ian pedantically – joking.

Jim shrugged and they both laughed.

Together, they surveyed the crowd.

The room was filled with all the usual suspects: academics with dandruffed shoulders, collectors who looked like their main passion was disappointing their grandchildren, and a spattering of dangerously rich hobbyists who could quote catalogue numbers better than they could recall their spouse's birthdays.

And there, by a case of Hungarian military stamps, stood the hatchet-faced man from Geneva.

He hadn't changed. Same pressed shirt, same unnerving stillness. A face like someone who judged dentists for not flossing properly. He wasn't looking at the stamps. He was once again looking directly at Ian.

Ian didn't flinch. He sipped his champagne, nodded at Jim, and turned away.

Once again Jim followed Hatchet Face. Ian waited at the Gala, feigning interest in a short lecture about wartime censorship in the Baltic postal services.

Eventually Ian's secure phone pinged.

"I'VE FOUND THEM. MEET ME AT 3 BELVEDERE GARDENS AS SOON AS YOU CAN. JIM"

When the coast was clear Ian went outside and hailed a cab and directed it to a quiet spot near Belvedere Gardens. Jim was already there, lurking in the shadows.

"He's not alone," Jim said, eyes narrowed. "I tailed him to a house just across the street," gesturing with his hand. "Then things got interesting."

He pulled out his phone and showed Ian a photo.

It was Duffy again. Malcolm bloody Duffy. In a cardigan, holding a reusable shopping bag, looking for all the world like a man popping out for eggs and a newspaper. And beside him?

The Bear Man.

Still enormous. Still terrifying. Still dressed like a mountaineer who moonlighted as a mob enforcer.

"Jesus," Ian muttered. "It's like the Antiques Roadshow crossed with a hostage situation."

The next day, they returned and scoped out the house further. Trying to work out the most efficient way to conduct a hit on Mr Duffy.

Duffy's house was a quaint, peach-coloured building on a quiet suburban street. The front garden had a small gnome, an aggressively trimmed hedge, and a welcome mat that read: "Ein Haus ohne Katze ist wie ein Himmel ohne Sterne."

Inside, visible through the window, was a horror show of ceramic Staffordshire dogs. They lined every shelf, crowded every sill. Ian counted at least thirty before he started to feel dizzy.

Oh, this was where Malcom Duffy lived alright thought Ian. Absolutely no doubt about it. Nobody else on earth had this level of obsession for ceramic dogs.

Jim and Ian watched. And waited.

Sometimes Hatchet Face would go out in a car – a gleaming black Škoda that looked suspiciously reinforced – for an hour's drive into the hills. Once, all three of them left together, laughing in what Ian described as "the way estate agents do just before scamming your grandmother," and disappeared for the better part of a day.

Every morning at exactly 10:17 a.m., like clockwork wound by malevolence and smugness, Mr Duffy, Hatchet

Face, and the Bear Man emerged from their ornate Viennese townhouse and ambled two streets over to *Café Grabenlust*, a popular haunt tucked between a tourist-trap Mozart wax museum and a boutique selling overpriced cuckoo clocks.

The café itself was achingly charming – wrought iron chairs, parasols striped like Neapolitan ice cream, and the lingering scent of sachertorte. The walls were ivy-covered, the staff disapproving, and the clientele a frothy mix of tourists, disaffected local students, and very quiet men reading very old newspapers.

Duffy and his two human-shaped shadows would sit at the same wrought iron table each day under a maroon parasol labelled *Julius Meinl – Seit 1862*, facing the square. Duffy drank black tea with lemon, always in a dainty china cup. Hatchet-Face preferred peppermint – no sugar, no expression. The Bear Man? He took a triple shot of espresso in a cup so small it looked like it belonged to a doll's tea set, but he sipped it with the solemnity of a man contemplating either war crimes or the meaning of life.

They'd sit precisely one hour. Never less. Rarely more. They hardly spoke, but when they did, it was in low tones and accompanied by facial expressions of mild amusement or disdain. Duffy's laugh was like a balloon deflating in slow motion. Polite, strangled, and somehow cruel.

On the third morning, Ian had decided. It was time to act.

"It's time," he told Jim, while buttering a croissant like he was waxing a rifle. "The planets have aligned. My bowel movements are regular. And frankly, I'm sick of watching that man sip tea like he's judging a piano recital."

Jim looked up from his surveillance monitor, which was cleverly disguised as an old copy of *Die Presse*. "You sure? If you miss, they'll vanish again."

Ian nodded. "I won't miss. I've got the crutch."

Ah yes – the crutch.

MI5's Vienna field office, operating out of a bland office above a schnitzel takeaway, had provided Ian with a Cold War relic repurposed by someone with a PhD in weaponry and deception. To the untrained eye, it was a medical walking aid. To the trained killer, it was a high-powered, bolt-action sniper rifle with a telescopic sight hidden inside the shaft. Twist twice, click, lock. Boom. Back to harmless orthopaedic accessory before anyone could cry "run!"

Ian had spent the previous afternoon on a derelict stretch of ground near Floridsdorf, testing it out. By the third shot, he was hitting old bratwurst tins at 200 metres. On the fifth, he split a peanut he had found in his jacket lining from a suspiciously long distance. Even Jim – best shot in his regiment – had been impressed.

"You hit that like a ninja with a nut allergy," Jim said, polishing his binoculars.

And so, the plan was simple. Ian would pose as an injured British tourist. He'd hobble toward the café opposite and sit at a table overlooking the target's usual spot, wait for Duffy to settle, and then – pop. Disappear into the flow behind the square. No CCTV. No chase. Clean and clinical.

The morning of the hit, Ian dressed the part. Checked scarf, thick-lensed glasses, a convincing fake limp, and a posture that screamed: "Ex-pat with gout." The rifle-crutch hung innocently from his wrist as he shuffled toward the café, nodding at pigeons like they were in on it. It was classic Cold War chic.

Jim took up his position across the square with a compact surveillance kit, small powerful binoculars and a chocolate croissant the size of a small child.

"You're in position, then?" Ian muttered through the comms hidden in his coat collar.

"Yup. Got you covered, mate. You look like a librarian's ghost."

Ian took that as a compliment.

He hobbled to a prime table – two down from a group of Finnish backpackers and just behind a couple trying to film an Instagram reel. He ordered a mineral water and pretended to wince while sitting. His eyes, however, were locked on *Table Seven* at *Café Grabenlust* – the one Duffy and crew had claimed every day.

And then he waited...

At exactly 10:17 a.m., as if summoned by the Gods, they arrived.

Duffy led, wearing a beige overcoat that screamed "retired dentist," followed by Hatchet Face, whose cheekbones looked freshly sharpened, and the Bear Man, who carried what might have been a potted plant or a small briefcase. Hard to tell with those enormous hands.

Ten more steps. Five. Three.

Duffy pulled out his chair. Hatchet Face nodded once at the waiter. The Bear Man placed the briefcase – no, it was definitely a briefcase – next to his seat and adjusted his napkin with all the delicacy of a man darning socks.

Ian's fingers tightened on the crutch. One twist. Two. The telescopic sight clicked into place with a tiny mechanical sigh. He shifted, lifted the rifle, sighted Duffy's neatly combed grey head in the crosshairs...

...and then the universe farted in his face.

A delivery lorry, massive and mustard-yellow, adorned with a cartoon bratwurst giving a thumbs-up, pulled directly into his line of sight. It wheezed to a stop in front of the café, disgorging steam and diesel with hydraulic vindictiveness. A man in shorts leapt down, began unloading boxes of "WürstKönig Deluxe," and continued to block Ian's view completely.

Ian swore. Loudly. In several languages. "Verdammter Wurstwagen!" he barked, drawing curious glances from nearby diners.

Jim spoke over comms. "Still got a line of sight?"

"Nope. I've got a line of a stuffing great mustard bratwurst truck, but not much else," Ian growled.

Ten painful minutes passed. The bratwurst man loaded boxes, rearranged them, checked a clipboard, then returned to his cab with all the urgency of a man painting a fresco. When the truck finally hissed and trundled off...

...Table Seven was empty.

Their cups sat in still life. Chairs were askew. But the men were gone.

Ian froze. Scanned the street. Nothing. No retreating backs. No car pulling away. Just the faint scent of peppermint tea and treachery in the air.

The Headhunter

Jim sighed in his earpiece. "Well. That went well."

Ian lowered the crutch and began to reassemble it into its faux-orthopaedic state, muttering obscenities under his breath.

"They must've clocked me," he said.

"Or," Jim countered, "they saw the bratwurst truck and thought it was a sign from the Gods to go home early."

Ian stood up, defeated but still weirdly hungry.

"Let's regroup," he said.

Ian looked into the clear blue sky, only to see yet another large bird of prey circling high above the café opposite.

"What is it with these birds," he thought?

Later, back at the hotel, Jim tossed Ian a can of cold beer from the minibar.

"I can't believe they slipped us again," he said.

Ian cracked open the beer and took a long swig.

"I bloody hate Vienna," he muttered.

Chapter Four
The Queen's Penny

"Never underestimate a quiet man with calloused hands."
~ CIA Operational Profile: "Type 7B" Agents
(Declassified 1994)

Chapter 4
The Queen's Penny

The Stamp Collector's Bulletin monthly content planner sat in Ian's inbox like a small, primed time bomb. As Editor-in-Chief, Ian took his responsibilities seriously. Which meant he outsourced most of them to a young intern, called Yassin, and then spent three hours designing an unnecessarily dramatic front cover entitled Tragedy and Perforation: The 1984 Alderney Misprint Scandal.

He had also chosen the theme for the next issue: Top Ten Sexiest Stamps You Shouldn't Lick in Public. Ruth of course did not approve.

When he was in the UK, Ian had begun working one day a week at the British Postal Museum & Archive. It was quiet, cool, and full of the sort of people who found punctuation erotic. It was also, crucially, somewhere to avoid Ruth's "catch-up chats" and close to a sandwich shop where they served Ian's favourite chicken escalope sandwiches, with sliced potato and melted cheese inserted between two slices of the most delicious fresh focaccia bread.

He made friends with Lorna, a volunteer who looked like she'd once seduced a vicar for access to a First Day Cover. She brought Ian 'Tunnock's Tea Cakes' and told him which cabinets were haunted, which he found strange yet slightly sweet.

"That one," she whispered, pointing at a mahogany display case. "Sometimes, it rattles when it's windy."

"Could be poltergeists," Ian said. "Or just bad joinery."

Lorna winked knowing. "Or a bit of both, maybe."

A message from Griffin arrived on Ian's encrypted phone whilst he was writing an in-depth article about commemorative Olympic stamp sets.

"NOVICH. RUSSIAN. POSTAL HISTORIAN. ASKING STRANGE QUESTIONS ABOUT YOU AND THE POSTAL MUSEUM. THINK HE IS PLANNING A VISIT SOON. SOMETHING SUSPICIOUS IS GOING ON. WATCH YOURSELF."

Ian deleted the message, stood up, and grabbed his coat. Time to go home.

Sure enough, a day later, Novich turned up unannounced at the Postal Museum.

Tall, sallow, early fifties. Balding in a manner that suggested he scratched his head a lot. He carried a satchel that looked suspiciously like it had been X-rayed a few too many times.

"I'm researching Cold War censorship techniques," Novich explained in smooth, polished English. "Specifically regarding aerogrammes and secret ink detection."

"Fascinating," Ian said, pretending to be a man who gave a toss. "Do you enjoy stamps, or just the espionage bits?"

Novich smiled thinly. "I am... fond of postal infrastructure."

Novich had wandered off somewhere deep in the labyrinthine bowels of the British Postal Museum. Ian, parked strategically on a bench had spent much of the intervening hours watching him on the CCTV feed.

When Novich eventually reappeared, he looked thoughtful. Too thoughtful for a man who'd spent two hours among commemorative stamp sets and decommissioned sorting machinery.

That night, over an aggressively late-night Scotch egg and some very suspect supermarket brandy, Ian reviewed further internal surveillance footage carefully. Novich had lingered far longer than necessary near the secure storage vault. He'd loitered near the Queen's Platinum Jubilee stamp plate, staring at it with a kind of religious awe. He'd asked Lorna – who had the vigilance of a sleepy vole – three increasingly specific questions about off-site transport protocols. He'd even taken notes. In a museum. On paper. With a fountain pen. Something was very definitely going on.

The next day, Novich returned. Same jacket. Same expression. Same weird fixation with the Queen's Platinum Jubilee plate, which he once again regarded with the reverence of a man meeting his long-lost twin. He seemed to be looking for something.

Ian decided it was time to accelerate things. To see if he could get to the bottom of things.

"Fancy a drink? I'd love to talk to you more" he asked, sidling up with the smoothness of a malfunctioning cement mixer. "There's a pub I know you might enjoy. Lots of dusty corners and stamp themed too."

Novich blinked. "A... stamp themed pub?"

"The Queen's Penny," Ian confirmed. "It's in Camden. Smells of postmen's uniforms and mail bags. You'll love it."

Novich, perhaps flattered or maybe merely intrigued, agreed.

That evening, under the flickering pub sign of a moustachioed Queen Victoria winking suggestively, they descended into the pungent gloom of The Queen's Penny. The walls were lined with battered red postboxes, moth-eaten postbags, and framed telegrams from forgotten wars. The bar was made of old railway sleepers, and the stools looked like they'd been stolen from a Scout hut in 1973.

Ian ordered pints of warm bitter, a bowl of pickled eggs, onions and olives that trembled when touched, and something the menu described only as "Postmaster's Surprise." This seemed to comprise large packets of thin pastry with what tasted like surprisingly dry shredded chicken inside.

Novich drank slowly, peering around the pub as if checking for escape routes. His hands never quite left his lap. His eyes flicked about like moths trapped in a lampshade.

Ian, by contrast, was expansive. Rambling. Disarming in the way only a man with access to national security protocols and a belly full of brine-soaked boiled eggs and onions could be.

"You know," he said, gesturing vaguely with a pickled egg, "there's a postcode in Wales that's just the letter L repeated six times. Even the postmen are confused."

Novich nodded slowly. "Fascinating."

"You ever licked a Penny Black?"

Novich gave him a narrow look. "That would be foolish. They are ungummed."

Ian grinned. "Just checking. It separates the philatelists from the fantasists."

He jabbed a large, oversized cocktail stick into a wayward onion and launched it toward his mouth like a harpoon. It missed. Bounced off his chest. Rolled down his shirt and into a crease of his trousers. Neither man mentioned it. He picked it out of his crutch as discretely as he could with his fingers and then popped it into his mouth.

After a couple of hours of drinking and talking about postal services through the Cold War period it was time to leave. Both men had run out of things to say and to be honest Ian was a bit bored with it all.

Outside, the air had that Camden tang – fried oil, cannabis, and whatever had died behind the kebab shop two months ago.

As they walked toward the underground station, Novich pulled out his phone to call someone. Ian pretended to not notice, admiring a puddle of water on the pavement.

Novich spoke in Russian. "Yes. He suspects nothing. I have the plate. Don't worry. We proceed tonight."

Ian paused, one eyebrow raised.

"Plate?" Ian said casually.

Novich turned. There was a fractional delay – not fear, not quite surprise – but the tick of a man whose brain was recalibrating options.

"I meant dinner plate. From a shop close to my office. It is... something a friend of mine asked me to secure for him."

"Mmm," Ian said, with theatrical disinterest. "I find ceramics uninspiring myself. Once knew a guy obsessed with Staffordshire dogs. Strange man."

They entered a narrow alley between a shuttered second-hand bookshop and a dubious tattoo parlour advertising "walk-in spiritual armpit sigils" in a flickering purple neon font. The air smelled of damp bricks, fryer oil, and mild criminality. A broken streetlamp buzzed overhead like a lazy wasp.

Novich slowed his pace. His eyes flicked left and right – the alley was empty, except for a pile of milk crates, a soggy mattress, and a graffitied bin that said "NEVER TRUST A PIGEON."

Ian stopped too. His tone was suddenly cheerful. "So," he said brightly, "just one last thing."

He saw it then – a twitch, a shift in weight, and Novich's hand sliding into his inner coat pocket.

Ian didn't hesitate. In one swift motion, he reached inside his own jacket and pulled free the absurdly long cocktail stick he'd pocketed earlier – the one he'd used to chase pickled onions around his plate in the pub. It still had a single small olive on it that Ian couldn't be bothered to eat, but thought he might have it later on the way home. It was a ridiculous thing – ten inches long, steel-core centre. One of those novelty cocktail skewers meant to look fun, but strong enough to impale an apple.

What most people didn't know is that if a sharp object enters the orbital cavity – the eye socket – at the right angle and with sufficient force, it will bypass the skull's protective bone structure and penetrate straight into the brain. A direct hit to the midbrain or thalamus could cause immediate catastrophic neurological shutdown. It didn't take a gun. It didn't even take much strength. Just precision. And a very long cocktail stick.

Ian drove it home.

With an awful *shluk*, it slid straight through Novich's right eye socket and deep into the brain tissue beyond. There was a half-second where Novich's body rebelled – flinching, twitching, his remaining eye wide with disbelief. His mouth made a tiny "oh" shape, like someone tasting lemon sorbet for the first time.

And then he collapsed like a deckchair kicked out from under a sunbather.

Ian grunted as he caught him – surprised by the dead weight of someone who looked so wiry. "Jesus, you're heavier than your moral compass," he muttered.

As he dragged him towards a nearby street bench, he felt Novich's fingers still twitching inside his jacket pocket. Curious, Ian reached inside – and his fingers closed around a small, cold object.

A handgun.

It was a compact Beretta 950 Jetfire – a tiny .25 ACP semi-automatic pistol, no larger than a Mars bar. Italian made, low recoil, eight-round magazine. The kind of weapon ideal for a covert agent with small hands and an eye for plausible deniability. Not powerful, but at close range? Lethal. And illegal in six countries. Straight from the assassin's playbook.

"Well, well," Ian murmured, sliding it smoothly into his own jacket pocket. "Someone came dressed for the occasion."

He sat Novich down gently on the bench like a sleepy commuter. He even adjusted the coat slightly, so it looked like Novich had simply dozed off after one too many sherries. The olive on the cocktail stick still poked from his eye socket like some grotesque canapé. Ian popped it back out. Spotting a nearby copy of the *Evening Standard* on the floor he picked it up and arranged the crumpled newspaper in Novich's hands and stepped back.

To passerby's, Novich looked like just another casualty of Camden's nightlife. But to Ian? He was a threat neutralised with precision, improvisation, and an olive garnish.

Ian rifled through the other pockets of Novich's jacket. And there it was: wrapped in tissue, slipped between two layers of bubble wrap was a printing plate. It was the smaller prototype plate for the Queen's Platinum Jubilee commemorative issue. Small. Relatively heavy for its size. Rare. Possibly priceless.

"That's legal tender, comrade," Ian muttered, slipping it into his coat like a souvenir from Brighton seafront.

Ian pulled out his secure phone and tapped a quick message to Griffin:

SUBJECT NEUTRALISED. PRINTING PLATE
RECOVERED. REQUEST DISCREET CLEAN-UP. BENCH:

CAMDEN, OPPOSITE SPIRITUAL ARMPITS. ALSO: SMALL HANDGUN RECOVERED. INTERESTING TOY. I'LL HAND IT OVER TO YOU WHEN I SEE YOU NEXT. IAN.

He turned and strolled down the alleyway, rolling his shoulders like a man who'd just cracked his neck after a long nap. As he passed a tattoo parlour, the door creaked open and a bored-looking man with glowing runes inked on his forearms gave Ian a polite nod.

"Nice night," the man said.

"A blind man would like to tell the difference," Ian replied, not breaking stride for a second.

Then, with all the casualness of a man late for his train, Ian wandered into a nearby pub toilet, flushed the cocktail stick – the murder weapon, washed his hands, and admired the graffiti. Someone had scrawled "Post Office: Delivering Disappointment Since 1660."

"Charming," Ian chuckled.

Then, like any good low level office worker finishing a very unconventional Tuesday evening, Ian adjusted his tie, patted his pocket to make sure the Beretta hadn't fallen out, and stepped out into the cold Camden air – whistling something that sounded suspiciously like *God Save the King* played backwards.

Ian sent a further message to Griffin.

SUGGEST YOU HAVE A LOOK AT THIS PRINTING PLATE TO SEE WHY HE MIGHT HAVE STOLEN IT.

Ian's phone pinged immediately

OK. ALL SOUNDS VERY SUPICIOUS. GRIFFIN.

With the adrenaline tapering off and the Camden air beginning to seep into his bones, Ian took the tube home, clutching a warm paper bag of fish and chips like it was a priceless heirloom. It smelt of grease, vinegar, and satisfaction. The Northern line was half-empty, save for a man dressed as a chicken and two French tourists arguing about Google Maps.

Home. North London. The gate squeaked as he opened it. Ian put his key in the door. Tolstoy launched himself at the door like a four-legged cannonball.

Inside, Susan was curled up on the sofa under a red furry blanket that Ian called her 'Narco-wrap'. A David Attenborough documentary about fungus was on TV. And Tolstoy barked loudly in welcome and sniffed Ian's hand.

The next morning dawned grey, wet, and apologetic.

Ian met Griffin in a grey Ford Mondeo parked behind a garden centre in Muswell Hill, north London. Classic MI5. Low profile. Low comfort. Smelt of mulch and government secrets.

Ian handed over the printing plate, so that the MI5 scientists and analysts could take a closer look. He also gave Griffin the small handgun.

"Cute little thing, perfect for 'plinking' in the back garden, was thinking of keeping it," Ian said. Griffin rolled his eyes and got into his car, driving off in the direction of the M25.

Later that night Ian got a message with a ping of his secure phone.

THAT PLATE...VERY INTERESTING. HAS A HIGHLY CLASSIFIED MICROFILE HIDDEN DEEP IN IT. SEEMS TO

HAVE SECRET INFORMATION ABOUT OUR NUCLEAR CAPABILITIES AND MISSLE SITES. ALSO, THE HANDGUN MATCHES SIX MURDERS OF AGENTS IN EUROPE. GOOD JOB. G.

Ian continued to report to work at the Post Office Headquarters in his usual blend of shambling dishevelment and disinterest. The office had never been quieter, and the only excitement was when someone accidentally ordered the wrong type of franking ink, or the photocopier broke down.

But Ian? Ian loved his wife and the familiar comfort of home, but he longed for something more. Not for the thrill. Not even for the danger. But for the comfortable hotel robes, heated toilet seats, and most of all for the enormous buffet breakfasts served by polite multilingual staff with very little regard for cholesterol.

He stared out the office window at a large feral London City pigeon pecking hopelessly at a Subway bag.

Soon, he thought. Soon, Daddy will fly again.

Chapter Five
Singapore Sling

"You can lie to your handler. You can lie to your mark. You can lie to your wife. Just don't lie to yourself. That's where mistakes get made."
~ MI5 Exit Interview, Agent X (last known words)

Chapter 5

Singapore Sling

Ian Taylor had lasted precisely twenty-seven days back in London before the itch returned. Not the usual one he blamed on a rogue brand of supermarket fabric softener, but the deeper, twitchier one that said: it's time to travel, lie shamelessly, eat 12,000 calories a day and probably kill someone in a hotel sauna. The ache for foreign espionage came with the scent of mini soaps, Danish pastries and mild jet lag.

Ian Taylor returned to Post Office Headquarters not with purpose, but with the languid reluctance of a man attending his own performance review after a stag weekend where you got drunk and were then tarred and feathered and left tied to a lamp post all night.

The reception area was its usual combination of laminated notices, the mild scent of boredom, and a security guard whose main skill appeared to be to stay looking excited and engaged when only eight people needed to be checked in throughout the entire day. Ian badge-swiped his way in, nodded at the variegated rubber plant he'd named "Steve" during a particularly boring tariff review meeting back in 2018, and took the lift to the first floor.

He didn't have a plan. He just needed to "show face," as Ruth had once ominously called it. And so he did, loitering around his desk like a reluctant ghost, walking around flapping a piece of paper, and occasionally tapping random keys in rapid, random bursts on his laptop to make it look like he was writing something confidential, or at the very least long and vital. He tapped the keys of his ancient laptop with the ratta-tat-tat of a machine gun. A grey-haired colleague, who had started at Post Office almost as long ago as Ian, had walked past – clearly impressed at Ian's work ethic, saying, "you are knocking it out this morning Ian."

Ian smiled appreciatively. "Thanks Pete, we do what we have to." he called out to Pete's disappearing back.

Ruth waved to him from her glassed-in managerial office with all the warmth of a woman who had once had hope and now had only budget responsibility. He waved back, mouthed something about "supply chain variance," and got a thumbs-up in return.

Bullshit baffles brains, Ian thought, laughing quietly to himself.

After twenty-three minutes of solid office theatre, he opened a Word document, wrote exactly one paragraph of his editorial for the *Stamp Collector's Bulletin*, entitled *"The Hidden Eroticism of Edwardian Cancellation Marks,"* and immediately closed his laptop with the flourish of a man who had delivered unto history something of vast intellectual weight and importance. That done, he slid on his battered coat and slipped away before anyone could ask him to attend a meeting, or to "jump on a call", or to "touch base."

Ian shot out of the building like a bullet.

27 minutes later, he was stepping through the battered doors of the launderette deep in the City, where the lighting was both too harsh and too flickery, and the smell suggested long-forgotten sandwiches and a lack of deodorant. The familiar hum of rotating machines created a mechanical lullaby of low-frequency despair. Pairs of socks tumbled in circles, each on a journey of slow-motion grief. The plastic chairs were cracked and no longer bothered trying to support anyone properly.

And there, as ever, was Griffin – folding a regulation-issue military bedsheet into aggressive thirds with the kind of precision usually reserved for mortuary prep. His face, chiselled from one of the sterner forms of granite, was impassive as ever. As always, he didn't look up.

"Singapore," he said, without pausing. "Philatelic conference. Big one. You're going to be a guest speaker."

Ian blinked. "Finally. My TED Talk moment. I'll need a clicker and some very dull, patronising slides."

Griffin ignored the comment and handed over a thick manila envelope sealed with red tape. Ian opened it. Inside: one glossy photo of a deeply unpleasant-looking man with a haircut that suggested government privilege and criminal tendencies; a printed itinerary that included disturbingly early morning panels; a plastic keycard to an upscale hotel;

and, perhaps most alarmingly, a laminated name badge identifying him as "Dr. Ian Caldwell-Taylor."

"You've got my name wrong?" Ian muttered, flipping the badge. "At least spell my name right. That's practically identity theft."

Griffin raised an eyebrow. "We thought it made you sound more important. You're lucky it doesn't say 'Philatelic Influencer.'"

"Don't tempt me. I'll start a YouTube channel. I can do it with Tolstoy. He can bark or slap his tail every time he agrees with me."

Griffin ignored him and continued. "Target is in the programme under the name Mr. Tan. Government liaison. Plausible diplomatic credentials. Real name's probably unpronounceable and classified. Triad ties so thick you could bind books with them," concluded Griffin, completely ignoring Ian's protestations about his name.

Ian looked again at the photo. "He looks like a man who eats gravel for breakfast."

"Our friends in the East want him gone. Quietly. No drama. No media. No Western footprint. And preferably not during the breakfast buffet."

"Of course," said Ian. "What do I look like? A savage?"

Griffin gave no reaction. "Weapons will be provided on arrival. Nothing traceable. Hotel staff are on side. Jim will be there already – he's going as an Australian stamp dealer specialising in marsupial commemoratives."

Ian winced. "Oh god. Will he be doing the accent?"

"Unfortunately, yes," confirmed Griffin with a pained look in his eye.

There was a moment. Griffin – who rarely indulged in anything beyond operational necessities – glanced up from his folding with something approaching warmth.

"How's the family?" he asked.

Ian shrugged. "They bought me a new GPS phone. I buried it in the garden by the hydrangea. I threw the trackable element into the back of a truck going to the West Country. Susan's convinced I have early-onset something. Possibly espionage-related dementia. Daisy's still in Belize. Apparently, her co-working hut has a hammock and an espresso bar. She sends me photos of sunsets and calls me a tosser."

Griffin allowed himself a short exhale. Not quite a laugh. Maybe a sigh in a dinner jacket.

"And Duffy?" Ian asked, voice shifting just slightly. "Any news?"

Griffin's entire posture hardened. The air between them changed.

"Gone again. Vienna was a near-miss, I know. But he's not gone-gone. We've got chatter. Movement in South America. Chile maybe. The phantom pottery dog collector's still at large. Don't you worry, we'll get him."

Ian's eyes narrowed. "Let me know when you've got something more concrete."

"You'll be the first."

There was a pause – long enough to be awkward, short enough not to require emotion.

"Right," said Ian. "Guess I better go home and iron my linen blazer and brush up on my knowledge about Singapore."

Griffin, still folding, didn't reply. He was already thinking of the next operative he had to brief later that day.

Ian pushed open the door of the launderette, stepping out into the chilly London afternoon. A pigeon landed on a traffic cone nearby, cooed once, and crapped on a Tesco bag.

Somewhere in his chest, Ian felt the familiar tingle of anticipation. Exotic hotel rooms. Questionable assassinations. Breakfast buffets that could change history.

He smiled.

Singapore was calling.

***

Three days later, Ian and Jim stepped into the air-conditioned splendour of the Singapura Intercontinental. The lobby was marble. The staff were perfect. The smell was part lemongrass, part generational wealth. Ian looked like a man who'd wandered in from a Post Office in Barnet and been mistaken for visiting royalty.

He was wearing a beige linen suit two sizes too large, knock-off Ray-Bans, and a tie featuring Queen Victoria winking. He tipped the bellboy in old Spanish Pesetas that he had found in the jacket's inner pocket and handed over his battered case with the wonky wheel, that weighed far more than it should have.

His room was on the 27th floor of the Imperial Synergy Resort, a terrifyingly upmarket hotel where everything looked like a movie set. The corner suite was a paean to excess: glass walls with a panoramic view of the Marina Bay Sands, carpets so thick Ian feared losing a shoe, and a toilet that required an engineering degree to operate. The bidet had a control panel resembling a fighter aircraft cockpit, complete with pressure settings, pulsation rhythms, and an emergency stop button.

The robes whispered old money and dry-cleaned privilege. The minibar practically shouted at him – full of gold-capped 18-year-old whisky miniatures, artisan peanuts harvested from volcanic soil, and what appeared to be a commemorative chocolate bar featuring Lee Kuan Yew.

Ian sat on the edge of the double emperor-sized bed – which could comfortably sleep a small Welsh village – and opened his dossier. His next target: Mr Tan. Smooth, charming, partial to vintage whisky, valuable stamps, and ancient Chinese calligraphy. Also: very well protected. Tan wasn't just rich – he was institutionally wealthy, with layers of state security, private guards, and deep state paranoia. Ian had 72 hours to make the man's demise look like natural causes. Ideally something with a high level of plausible deniability. Or a very bad case of indigestion.

There was a knock. Ian padded over in his hotel slippers, and luxury towelling dressing gown – which looked two sizes too small for him – and opened the door.

Jim stood there holding a small paper bag. "Room service," he said.

Ian took it and peeked inside. A packet of Tic Tac mints. "Ooooh mints!"

"Laced with a refined form of hemlock. Won't kill him immediately. But a handful of those and he'll experience gentle cardiac shutdown. Quick, discreet, just a whiff of 'he should've drunk more water.'"

"Classy," Ian said. "You know how to treat a lady."

"He apparently has a real weakness for small mints. Just don't forget and help yourself to a handful," said Jim. "They are your loaded gun."

Jim flopped into a nearby armchair and grabbed a handful of artisan nuts from a fancy jar above the minibar. "Three days of conference hell. You going to be okay in there?"

"I once spent a week at a conference about postal automation in Cleethorpes. This is utter paradise my friend."

***

Day One of the 'East meets West' International Philatelic Conference opened with all the theatre of a small-town mayoral inauguration. The conference hall – chandeliered, over-air-conditioned, and faintly buzzing with the scent of collector-grade polyester – was already heaving. Men with lanyards shuffled through the exhibit booths like ghosts armed with tote bags. There were murmured arguments about postmarks, quiet gasps at rare misprints, and one grey haired man with a goatee beard quietly sobbing over a misplaced perforation.

Ian surveyed it all like a butcher at a vegan buffet. With professional detachment, mild horror, and the suspicion that someone near him had wet themselves with joy over a misprint.

He gave a speech that morning entitled: "Modern Marketing Strategies for Se-Tenant Stamps: The Unsung Heroes of Perforated Philately." It was part nonsense, part fact, part ignorance. One man shook his head in disagreement throughout. Another attempted to record it but dropped his phone into his tea. At least two people nodded off, and someone – Ian suspected a Canadian – snored gently.

After the speech, Ian wandered the booths. The Japanese minis. The Cuban overprints. The Moldovan commemoratives. And then Ian saw him.

Mr Tan. Elegant in a cream linen suit and tortoiseshell glasses. Admiring a 1971 Osaka Expo commemorative with the attention of a jeweller inspecting a fine diamond.

"Lovely borders," Ian offered.

Mr Tan turned. "The best are subtle," he replied, smiling faintly.

Their eyes met. It wasn't love. But it was... comfort. Familiarity. Ian felt something strange stir in his gut. Not curry. Not paranoia. Something resembling affection of some kind... well at least recognition of his fellow man of some sort. He'd read about bromances in the paper once. Maybe this was one of those. And Mr Tan seemed to be vibing right back at Ian.

They talked for an hour. Tan was a man of stories. He spoke of his childhood, his love of maritime airmail, and a particular stamp from Bhutan that played the national anthem when licked. Ian, despite himself, liked him. It was going to be difficult killing him Ian thought.

"Coffee?" Ian asked.

"Why not?" Tan replied.

They strolled through the tropical gardens. Past koi ponds and billion-dollar orchids. They drank espresso in a quiet terrace café, surrounded by conference delegates arguing about the over commercialisation of stamp issues.

Ian found himself relaxed. Enjoying the company.

Later, as they sat watching koi fish that probably had names and trust funds, Ian reached into his pocket.

"Mint?" asked Ian, offering the packet of Tic Tacs to Tan.

Tan took two. "Oooh! Tic Tacs! My favourite."

He popped them in his mouth. Chewed thoughtfully. Smiled.

"Here, have a couple more," said Ian helpfully.

They strolled around a bit more, like old friends, and then Mr Tan announced, "I'm feeling a bit tired, I think I'll retire to my room for a while. Maybe we could have dinner one evening before you go back to London."

"That would be wonderful," replied Ian slightly doubtfully that Mr Tan was going to be having dinner anytime soon.

The next morning Ian watched Mr Tan's covered body being wheeled out to an Ambulance.

The medical report cited *natural causes* – mild dehydration and a peculiar minty aroma. Ian toasted the news with a lavish champagne breakfast, while doing a crossword in the infinity pool.

Jim joined him, towel slung over his shoulder, flip-flops flapping like a weary pelican.

"Blimey," Jim said, eyeing the champagne in Ian's hand. "That was quick. You didn't hang about! We're still booked in for two more days."

Ian shrugged with the contentment of a python post-feast. "Be a shame to waste it. I'm due at the chocolate buffet in twenty minutes."

"Chocolate buffet?" Jim raised both eyebrows, eyes wide.

"Floor 14. Swiss-trained pâtissiers. Twenty-seven types of truffle. One of them comes in a little gold box."

Jim blinked. "I was just going to try the steam room."

"Amateur," Ian said, standing up with a groan and a crackle of joints that sounded like someone stepping on bubble wrap.

And so, they stayed.

Ian gorged on luxury with the fervour of a man whose idea of self-care back home was microwaving baked beans directly in the tin. He ordered pillow menus with a serious expression, tried every bath salt offered in the spa, and insisted on wearing two robes at once "for temperature layering."

Jim discovered the hotel's cigar lounge, a mahogany paradise where oil barons and retired mercenaries exchanged Latin quotes and whisky recommendations. He fitted in disturbingly well.

Ian and Jim hit the rooftop bar and made loud, inappropriate toasts to philately, espionage, and the enduring utility of elasticated waistbands.

"May all your postmarks be commemorative!" Ian bellowed at one point, sloshing a plume of vintage champagne up the back of an investment banker from Dubai.

At one point in the proceedings Ian entered the spa's meditation suite, fell asleep during guided breathing, and woke up two hours later with cucumber slices fused to his eyelids.

He entered a tai chi class by mistake and stayed, convinced it was interpretive martial arts. The instructor gave up trying to correct him after Ian shouted "SHAOLIN!" during a slow breathing sequence and attempted a cartwheel that ended in tears and a damaged Achilles tendon.

Ian and Jim both ate like warlords. Peking duck with mango glaze. Lobster dumplings served in miniature steam trains. A deconstructed tiramisu that took fifteen minutes to reassemble and three seconds to inhale.

On day three, Ian took a final dip in the infinity pool, drifting like a bloated croissant in warm chlorine, solving a Times crossword while balancing a plate of gyoza on his chest.

He also wrote a poem in the spa relaxation room for Susan. It was terrible. Truly dire. But it rhymed:

O Singapore, your towels are thick,
Your breakfast spreads are huge and slick,
I came to kill, and that I did,
Now pass the prawns and lift the lid.

Jim clapped. The therapist just looked bewildered, putting down her lack of understanding to English not being her native tongue.

That evening, they ventured out to a highly exclusive restaurant – The Celestial Lychee, nestled atop a converted art gallery overlooking the harbour. The menu had no prices. The waiters wore tuxedos. The wine list came in a leather-bound binder thicker than the MI5 code of conduct.

Ian caused a minor diplomatic incident when, overwhelmed by the opulence and the twelve separate pieces of cutlery, he belched during a toast by the Saudi ambassador and then laughed so hard he knocked over a decorative bonsai tree into a French diplomat's consommé.

"Sorry, old boy," he said, attempting to mop up the soup with the ambassador's napkin. "Bit gassy. Too much sashimi foam."

"Sir," the maître d' hissed, "this is a delicate establishment."

"Tell that to my intestines," Ian replied, before vanishing into the lavatory with the velocity of a flushed pheasant.

Later, in the lobby, still reeling from fish mousse and fermented lotus root, Ian sat on a velvet pouffe and stared into the glinting chandelier above.

He reached into his pocket and pulled out his personal 'old school' phone. He tapped a short message to Susan.

Still alive. Miss your lentil bake. Love you, Mummy. x

Then another.

P.S. I think I'm officially too old for international gourmet assassination.

Her reply arrived an hour later:

Are you drunk, Daddy?

"No, just missing you Mummy," he replied.

"I'm missing you too, Daddy."

He smiled, closed his eyes, and allowed himself – for the first time in a while – to feel something dangerously close to happiness.

When their flight finally loomed, Ian sighed with the melancholy of a man leaving behind a lifestyle he could neither afford nor digest ever again.

As he waddled towards the airport gate, bloated on the successful destruction of 40,000 calories of high-end gourmet food, and self-reflection, Jim patted him on the shoulder.

"Good trip?"

Ian grunted. "I think I've gained a stone, a conscience, and possibly type two diabetes."

"Let's never tell anyone how nice this was," he said.

Jim raised his champagne glass. "To stamp collecting. And silence."

They clinked glasses. And watched the Singapore skyline burn gold in the setting sun.

Once on the plane Ian reached into his pocket to see if he could find an indigestion tablet. Instead, his fingers brushed something waxy and flat.

A folded piece of parchment like card. Old-fashioned. Handwritten in ink – rather like calligraphy. Smelt of lavender.

You missing me? D.

Beneath it, a wax seal: a relief image of Staffordshire spaniel.

Ian stared at the note.

Duffy! Bloody Duffy! He's bloody playing with me, thought Ian. The bastard!

He reached for his hip flask. He swigged at it aggressively and got out his laptop. He had a lot of time to kill on this flight.

Time to write the 'A word from the Editor' section of the Stamp Collectors Bulletin for next month.

Chapter Six
The Librarian

"If in doubt, blame a rogue faction and change your accent."
~ **CIA Crisis Manual, Volume III**

Chapter 6

The Librarian

Ian Taylor often felt that Brussels was a place that looked like someone had started building a fairy tale and then stopped halfway through to do a lot of admin. There was beauty, yes - in the curling stone gargoyles, the towering spires, the scent of waffles and rotisserie chickens wafting through the damp air - but it was also a city of bureaucracy, indecision, and suspiciously powerful mayors.

Ian had checked into the Hôtel des Archives, a grimly polite five-star hotel that overlooked the square near Place du Jeu de Balle, where on a Sunday stamp dealers spread their collections across folding tables with the reverence of medieval priests laying out relics. Ian's room had high ceilings, whispering curtains, and a minibar that looked like it had last been updated during the Cold War.

He arrived under his usual civilian cover: scruffy, slightly unwashed, disgruntled Post Office middle-level manager on a "cultural exchange of philatelic knowledge." The Belgian hosts didn't care. As long as you paid the hotel bill and didn't urinate in the lift, you could call yourself anything you liked.

That morning, Ian sat with a stale croissant and strong black coffee in the hotel restaurant, reading the file Griffin had slid across a washing machine at the launderette two days earlier. Codename: The Librarian. Real name unknown. Ex-KGB. Archivist, turned information broker, turned serious thorn in NATO's collective backside. Fond of rare books, esoteric stamps, and creating personal data empires from the inside out. Ian pictured a tweedy man surrounded by dusty tomes and slightly illegal USB sticks. The file suggested he was responsible for leaking the locations of refugee safehouses across Europe. People had died. Kids, even. This wasn't about cover stories or tidy wet-work. This one mattered.

"And the bastard has an executive level membership card for the Royal Belgian Philatelic Society," Ian muttered.

His cover? An invite-only sub-expo held in the catacombs below the official collector's market. It wasn't listed on any agenda. But if you knew the right handshakes and dropped enough Latin stamp terminology, you could buy a used Napoleon III envelope, three counterfeit Greek intelligence maps, and an entire Belgian civil servant's inbox on a memory stick – all before elevenses.

Ian dressed for the part: thick glasses, beige mac, tie featuring a Penny Black. He completed the look with an obnoxiously large stamp album and a Belgian flag pin. It screamed: obsessive, lonely, probably harmless. Which, as Ian knew, was precisely the way to ensure that people underestimate you.

The Headhunter

The underground market was nestled behind a shuttered Metro entrance near Rue Blaes. Ian walked through a discreet gate disguised as a janitor's closet, down stone steps soaked with generations of rain and secrets. Inside, the market buzzed with coded chatter. Fluorescent lights flickered overhead. Fold-out tables held stamps, war bonds, seditious leaflets, passports, and occasionally bloodied cash.

"Looking for the Moldovan misprints," Ian told the vendor at stall 42, as instructed.

The man nodded, reached under the table, and handed him a pass stamped with a cockerel and an owl. Ian tucked it inside his jacket. That was the invitation he need to gain access.

Down a further hallway, past crates of rotting paperbacks and a drunk man whispering "Gibraltar overprints" into a payphone, was a steel door. Ian knocked twice, waited, knocked once. The door creaked open.

Inside, the air smelt of mould, ink, and something slightly electrical. The Librarian's private salon.

The Librarian was smaller than Ian expected. Neat. Bald. Fastidious. His voice was flat as an e-reader, his handshake disturbingly cold.

"You are interested in postal anomalies?"

"Who isn't?" Ian replied.

"Come. I have something for you."

The room behind him was lined with bookshelves – not ordinary books, but dossiers. Intelligence clippings, printed chat logs, lists of embassy deliveries and intercepted parcels. The stamps were a front. The real collection was power, bound in A4.

Ian kept up the charade. They talked stamps, discussed French colonial errors, and debated over-inking techniques in mid-70s Tunisia. Then, the Librarian excused himself to retrieve something "special."

That's when Ian moved.

He opened drawers. Snapped a few phone shots. In the bottom filing cabinet, under a false partition, he found it: a ledger.

Names, locations, dates.

One page flagged operations carried out in Vienna, Prague, Manchester, Jakarta. The signatures were mostly code-names. But one page was different. At the top: *DUFFY.*

Under it, in spidery ink, were lines of linked operations. Small-time at first: surveillance, asset testing, psychological manipulation. Then darker: double agents. Torture. Chemical testing. Murder.

Ian flipped the page.

One name stood out. *SUSAN TAYLOR.*

His wife.

Her name was circled in red ink. And under it, three words: "Conditioned. Observed. Useful."

Ian felt the ground tilt. It wasn't just leverage. She was part of something.

The door creaked.

Ian dropped the book back into place, straightened his tie, and smiled.

The Librarian entered, holding a folder. "A rare Peruvian charity issue," he said.

"Wonderful," Ian replied. "Tell me – do you have anything from Patagonia?"

The Librarian's face flickered.

Seconds later, Ian flipped the table and drove a commemorative Queen's Jubilee Biro into the man's neck. A gurgle. Blood ran like a river. A thud.

The folder fell to the floor. Inside was a photograph of Duffy. Standing in a north London garden. Smiling.

Ian grabbed the photo, the ledger, and torched the rest.

Fire soon took hold and raced through the entire building – burning everything in its path to a fine ash.

Outside, Brussels carried on as if nothing had happened. Ian walked back to the hotel through drizzling streets, heart thudding.

Ian quickly sent a message to Griffin.

JOB DONE: TARGET CLEAN. NO EXPOSURE. PACKAGE SECURE.

Ian stared out at the rainy street. Somewhere, Malcolm Duffy was still out there. Watching. Plotting. And Susan... Susan was now somehow involved.

He didn't know why or how yet. But he would find out.

Even if it killed him.

Chapter Seven
Return to Sender

"Espionage is 20% intelligence, 30% paperwork, and 50% lying convincingly to your spouse."
~ **Unofficial field notes, Canadian Security Intelligence Service (CSIS)**

Chapter 7

Return to Sender

Ian was glad to be home. Genuinely glad. And that was rare for a man who had recently preferred room service to conversation, and foreign hotels to familiar domesticity. But after Geneva and Singapore – after Duffy's sudden reappearance and the business with the poisoned mints – something had shifted.

He'd missed Susan. And Max. Even Daisy, though she mostly communicated via emojis, WhatsApp messages and grainy sun-drenched updates from remote locations. There was a comfort in the egg-stained mundanity that Ian now found himself oddly craving. Tea with real milk. The smell of dirty laundry. The thud of Tolstoy's tail whenever someone mentioned the word 'sausages' or 'walk'.

But beneath the calm, Ian felt it – that tickle at the back of his neck. The one that usually meant someone was watching. Or about to try and neutralise him. Or both.

The day began, as many of Ian Taylor's more regrettable days did, with a sense of creeping unease, mild dread, and a jar of kimchi that looked like it might file a lawsuit.

He stood in the kitchen, fork in hand, staring down the fermented cabbage like it had insulted his mother. The label was in Korean, the date partially rubbed off, and the lid hissed when opened in a way that felt legally actionable.

Tolstoy, sprawled on the kitchen tiles like a dark sentient bathmat, thumped his tail twice and fixed Ian with a look of cautious encouragement. He was always up for a challenge, especially edible ones. How bad could kimchi really be?

Ian dipped the fork in.

Then thought better of it.

He opted instead for a breakfast made of mild desperation and any leftovers he could get his hands on: half a slice of ham, a dollop of low-fat Greek yoghurt scraped from the lid, and three pickled gherkins – one of which had mysteriously grown a hair. It was a long way from the recent glory days of Geneva and Singapore. How the mighty had fallen Ian thought to himself. But it was home and felt reassuringly safe.

He was halfway through assembling this eclectic selection of leftovers into something resembling a 'bowl' when his phone buzzed. Not the buzz of his ancient personal Nokia – which mostly communicated nagging reminders from Susan or promotional texts from Specsavers.

No. This was the *other* one. The secret encrypted one

Ian flipped it open.

Griffin: Target active. Duffy's moving again. Confirmation that Susan may be exposed. You need to move her. Details to follow. Get to the penthouse and we can arrange everything as a priority today.

For a second, Ian just froze.

The kitchen, with its half-peeled banana on the counter, the fridge humming its mournful note, and Tolstoy now licking the outside of the yoghurt pot Ian had dropped onto the floor, faded away.

Susan.

He could take being hunted. Shot at. Possibly poisoned. Even accidentally enrolled for two separate health insurance medicals in the same week. But *not* his wife. *Not* his children.

With the urgency of a man who had just remembered where he left a candle burning, Ian sprang into action.

Ten minutes later, he was out of the door in what might have generously been described as "combat casual." Combat trousers from the 90s (probably unwashed since Kosovo), a faded T-shirt featuring the slogan *"Ask Me About Stamps"* now adorned with a squashed baked bean in the shape of Albania, and a hoodie that smelt of mustard.

He left Tolstoy with half a tin of sardines and a command to "guard the perimeter" – which the dog interpreted as "eat this and nap for three hours."

Ian bolted to his 'safe house' – or more specifically his safe luxury penthouse apartment with all the mod-cons, weapon arsenal and disguise cupboard, known only to four people and one pizza delivery driver with no sense of security clearance. Key-coded. Bug-proofed. Stocked with

Havana cigars, fine scotch, espionage gear, gadgets galore and three unopened bottles of celebratory Bollinger he kept forgetting to drink.

He sat at the luxurious uncluttered modern desk and opened a secure emergency comms channel on a sleek, modern, encrypted laptop with Griffin.

"Griffin," he barked. "Talk to me."

The screen flickered. Then, Griffin's gruff, scowling face appeared. He looked like someone who had never really ever smiled and didn't intend to start now.

"She's been flagged," Griffin said. "We intercepted a transmission routed through a dark web exchange. Susan's name came up. So did Daisy's. Nothing specific yet, but Duffy's patterns are changing. He's not just dodging us. He's circling. It confirms what you uncovered in the file you secured in Brussels."

Ian felt his gut twist. And not just because of the gherkins.

"Why now?" he said.

"Pressure. You are getting close. That plate you took off Novich in Camden – you've rattled a few cages recently. We're working the backchannels, but Duffy's gone personal on you. He's not just trying to get away anymore. He wants to hurt you. Cripple you. Take you out. And your family. He wants to make a point."

Ian stood, walked to the reinforced window, and looked out over the city skyline. Rain pattered softly on the glass. Below, London moved with its usual indifference – black cabs crawling, joggers running, a Deliveroo driver fighting with a rogue bin bag.

The Headhunter

"Send a team," Ian said. "I want eyes on the house. On Max. On Daisy too – she is still in Belize. She'll need to be brought back. Good luck with that. Subtle. Nothing flashy."

"We're on it," Griffin said, his voice flat as ever. "But you know the drill. If this escalates…"

"I know," Ian interrupted. "Gloves off. Teeth out. Full John le Carré."

The video call ended with a soft click. The screen went blank. The silence that followed felt heavier than it should.

Ian stared at the screen for a moment, then leaned back in his Bauhaus chair. He opened a drawer – a shallow one, there were two Mont Blanc pens – one an ink pen and one a ball point, a half-finished packet of Murray Mints, and beneath it all, a photograph.

Susan. Laughing. Caught mid-sentence, hair tied back, a strand escaping to curl across her cheek. The kind of smile you couldn't fake. The kind of woman who could terrify a council subcommittee with a look and still get home in time to cook a pasta bake and rearrange the cereal cupboard alphabetically.

He looked at the photograph longer than he intended. Then muttered, under his breath, "Time to deliver."

He grabbed his encrypted phone and tapped a message to Griffin:

WHAT DO I TELL THEM? HOW DO I EXPLAIN ALL OF THIS TO THEM?

The reply came back almost immediately:

MAYBE JUST TELL HER THE TRUTH!

Ian snorted audibly. His thumbs flew across the keypad in a frenzy.

WHAT? THAT I'M A SECRET ASSASSIN POSING AS AN INEPT, SLIGHTLY STINKY, POST OFFICE WORKER? THAT I'VE BEEN SILENTLY BUMPING OFF FOREIGN OPERATIVES, WAR CRIMINALS AND ARMS DEALERS BETWEEN STAMP SYMPOSIA? THAT I HAVE MORE SECRET BANK ACCOUNTS THAN HSBC BANK? AND, OH YES – THAT OUR FORMER NEIGHBOUR IS TRYING TO KILL ME, HER AND OUR KIDS?

There was a pause.

Then:

WELL, MAYBE NOT *ALL* OF IT THEN.

Ian could feel the vein in his temple beginning to throb.

WELL, WHICH BLOODY BITS DO YOU SUGGEST?! he typed furiously.

Griffin replied with the calm of a man whose job was stress, distilled:

TELL HER YOU WERE APPROACHED BY MI5 TO REPORT BACK FROM SOME OF YOUR PHILATELIC EVENTS. ONE PERSON TOOK EXCEPTION TO THIS. HE'S MADE A THREAT. WE'RE TAKING IT VERY SERIOUSLY. IT'S A TEMPORARY SECURITY RELOCATION JUST TO BE ON THE SAFE SIDE.

Ian exhaled slowly through his nose.

OK. WHERE ARE YOU TAKING US? he typed.

COTSWOLDS. SMALL EXCLUSIVE HOTEL. LUXURY SPA. SECURITY DETAIL DISGUISED AS YOGA INSTRUCTORS. BUFFET BREAKFAST RATED FIVE STARS BY THE AA. HAVE MAX AND SUSAN READY AT 20:00, G.

COPY THAT, concluded Ian, realising that panicking wasn't going to help anyone.

Ian returned the picture of Susan to its rightful place, shut the drawer of his desk, grabbed his coat, and left the penthouse at a pace not seen since the ninja star incident in Prague over 11 years earlier. He was halfway home before he realised he'd been muttering "pasta bake, pasta bake, pasta bake" under his breath like a calming meditative mantra. Ian decided to stop this compulsive behaviour by saying "release the mantra," loudly to himself in public. This got him a lot of bemused looks on the train he was travelling on but stopped him losing all control of his bodily functions.

By the time he reached his front door, his stomach had twisted itself into a complex sailor's knot. He felt like he was on the brink of a panic attack. He paused on the step. Took another very deep breath. Considered vomiting into the Camilia in the front garden. He then unlocked the front door and walked in.

Even the dog seemed surprised Ian was home before the 5 o'clock news.

Tolstoy met him like a large fur-covered truck, barking once and banging his tail so hard against the radiator it made a sound like a church bell being struck with a marrow at a village fete.

Susan appeared at the end of the hallway, wiping her hands on a tea towel. She looked vaguely suspicious, in the way only a woman who knows your every tick and tremor can.

"Well, this is unexpected," she said, wide eyed. "Home before nightfall. What have we done to deserve this?"

"I... I have news," Ian said, forcing a smile that felt like it had been glued on backwards.

Susan narrowed her eyes. "You aren't having an affair, are you?" she asked. "You haven't got someone at work pregnant, have you?"

"No. But... erm... well...erm... we've won a prize," he stuttered out in a panic.

"A prize?"

"A luxury holiday. In the Cotswolds. Two weeks. Spa. Countryside. All expenses paid. They even do hot-stone treatments and freshly squeezed beetroot juice. Which I personally find disgusting, but it's meant to be good for the spleen."

Susan stared at him. "You entered a competition?"

"Yes! Kinda!" Ian said brightly. "Through work. You know. Post Office... morale initiative, that type of thing," he lied.

"Since when do you win anything?"

"Well, I have been putting a lot of good karma out into the universe lately."

"Really?"

"Yes. I recycled a yoghurt pot last week."

Tolstoy sneezed.

"When do we go? I'll need to buy some new clothes," said Susan starting to like the sound of this. "I haven't got a thing to wear."

"Tonight," answered Ian as if this was the most obvious answer in the world.

"Tonight?!" said Susan almost in a shout. "Are you bloody off your rocker, Daddy?"

"Yes tonight," confirmed Ian. "I told you it was a surprise."

Susan crossed her arms. "A surprise? A bloody surprise? And we have to go *tonight*?"

"It's a very exclusive window. Like that restaurant that only opens for three hours every solstice."

"Right," she said slowly, "and I assume someone will come to collect us, or do we have to drive ourselves?"

"Oh no. An executive coach of some sort. Coming to pick us up. Very classy. Cup holders and everything."

Susan gave him that look. The one that could pierce armour plating.

Ian tried a softer approach. He stepped closer. "Listen," he said quietly. "I just want to take you somewhere peaceful. Away from all the... bins and bills. Somewhere safe. Spend some quality time together – after all my recent travel. Somewhere lovely where we can really reconnect."

Susan's expression softened. Only slightly.

"And there's a hot tub," Ian added. "And possibly a man named Gavin who does reflexology."

She sighed. "Fine. But I'm packing my own pillow and I'm not meditating in a yurt."

"Deal," agreed Ian – while he was ahead.

As she turned to head upstairs to pack, Ian messaged Griffin again.

SHE BOUGHT IT. MOSTLY. PLEASE TELL ME GAVIN IS REAL.

Griffin's reply:

WE HAVE TWO GAVINS. ONE'S A DECOY. OTHER ONE IS EX-MI6 AND DOES AMAZING LAVA STONE WORK.

Ian closed the phone, looked up the stairs, and said to himself:

"Right. Let's keep this family alive... and possibly exfoliated while we are about it."

Susan didn't quite know what to make of it. But she packed, as she always did, with tidy efficiency and tightly controlled scepticism. She hauled down two weathered suitcases from the loft, the kind with tags from pre-baggage-charge holidays. Max grumbled theatrically as he was instructed to fold clothes, muttering something about being in the middle of watching a documentary about the Taliban.

By the time the clock ticked to 20:00 exactly, the street outside their North London home was bathed in the soft glow of sodium lamps and the muffled thump of Tolstoy barking like a canine possessed.

Then came the knock. Three short, deliberate raps.

At this, Tolstoy launched into full war-dog mode, his tail thudding like a bass drum against the hallway radiator.

Ian opened the door to reveal Griffin, looking very much like a man who'd already had quite enough of the evening, flanked by two impossibly broad men in expensive dark suits and reflective Ray-Bans – despite the fact it was now already completely dark.

Susan's expression flickered from polite curiosity to open suspicion.

"This... isn't a coach," she said flatly, looking out of the window at the car that had come to collect them.

"No," Ian said. "Change of plans. Executive upgrade."

Griffin cut in, pulling Ian to one side in the hall. "Have you told her?"

"I told her we have won a prize," Ian replied sheepishly, "She thinks it's a wellness holiday."

Griffin groaned. "You useless bastard."

Tolstoy tried to dry mount one of the security men. The man didn't flinch.

"Come on," Griffin snapped. "Lock up the house and get in the bloody car."

Ian gave the front door one last apologetic glance, farted under the strain of twisting the old mortice lock, and shuffled towards the imposing navy-blue Range Rover now idling in the street. It had blacked-out windows, an odour of expensive leather, and an aura of diplomatic immunity.

Susan narrowed her eyes but climbed in. So did Max.

The Range Rover pulled smoothly away from the kerb. It glided rather than drove – effortlessly powerful, cocooning them from the outside world with that unnerving quiet only serious vehicles ever manage. No radio. No chatter. Just the occasional squawk of Griffin's comms system and the low thrum of the V8 engine.

Two further almost identical Range Rovers joined them, one at the front, one behind – full of large men with hard stares and dark glasses.

Susan stared out the window, watching familiar London dissolve into countryside at an oddly rapid pace. "Why are we being waved through traffic?" she asked, peering as police officers cleared junctions ahead of them like a royal motorcade.

Ian tried to ignore her, pretending he hadn't heard.

Max leaned forward. "Mum, I think Dad's involved in something illegal."

"No talking," Ian said quickly. "Or breathing too loudly."

"OMG, we are being taken into witness protection," announced Max dramatically.

The fields were dark. The sat-nav softly whispered incomprehensible village names. By the time they reached Gloucestershire proper, the trees had thickened and the stars were visible in a clear ink black sky.

Eventually, a few hours later, they turned off the road through high wrought-iron gates and onto a gravel drive lined with lanterns. The sign read:

Hedgerose Hall – A Sanctuary for the Senses

Susan blinked. "This looks... expensive."

"It's a special, very exclusive, off-season," Ian said, which was true in the sense that it was just for them with no other guests, guarded by about a dozen specially trained MI5 agents.

As they arrived, the drive curved to reveal an opulent manor house – part stately home, part Bond villain lair. There were staff lined up outside in perfectly pressed uniforms. Bellhops with clipboard precision. And, oddly, several more very large men in smart suits and dark glasses speaking quietly into earpieces while pretending to water plants and rearrange the sun loungers.

"Are they expecting someone important?" Max asked, eyeing a man with a sidearm not-so-subtly tucked beneath his jacket.

"Just us," Ian said, wincing internally.

They were met on the steps by a tall, elegant woman in a silk scarf and heels that didn't belong anywhere near gravel.

"Welcome to Hedgerose Hall," she said warmly. "We're honoured to host you. Your suite... in fact the hotel... is ready for you."

Ian mouthed a silent "thank you" to Griffin, who then disappeared somewhere behind the security perimeter.

Their suite was something out of a Scandinavian design magazine if the magazine had been sponsored by royal palaces. A fire flickered in a marble hearth. Towels were shaped like swans on a bed big enough to host a UN summit. In the en-suite, a sunken bath large enough for Tolstoy to swim in, slap bang in the centre of the room beneath a skylight.

Susan stood in awe. "Well," she said slowly, "this is... some place."

She wrapped her arms around Ian. "Thank you. I don't know how you've pulled this off. But I'll take it."

Ian smiled, basking for a fleeting moment in her approval. "All in a day's work."

Then, softly, she added, "Now tell me what's really going on. Are you really a Mafia boss or something?"

The words dropped like a pebble in an icy pond.

Ian froze.

"I... what do you mean?" he asked, voice several octaves too high.

Susan raised an eyebrow. "Ian, there are men outside with military haircuts and muscle tone that doesn't come from pilates. No one wins a surprise trip to a luxury spa at 8 p.m. escorted by men in sunglasses at night. You don't even play the lottery."

Ian looked at her. She wasn't angry. She wasn't panicked. Just... calmly waiting for the lie to end.

He sighed and sat on the bed.

"Okay," he said. "There might have been a bit more to this than me winning a bloody prize."

"Go on," said Susan. "You might as well just tell me the truth."

"I may have... accidentally crossed paths with a dangerous man. He's made some threats. MI5 thinks it's best you and Max aren't at home for a few days."

Susan blinked. "MI5?"

"Technically I've been assisting them... under cover... there are lots of things I can't tell you – so please don't ask... erm...maybe one day. Official Secrets Act and all that."

"Jesus Christ, Ian."

"I didn't want you involved," said Ian.

"You've dragged me out of my own kitchen... at night, Ian. I am bloody involved."

"I was trying to keep you safe."

Susan stood in silence. Then sat down next to him. "Is it really that serious?"

"Yes."

"And you've been doing this the whole time? While pretending to review cancellation marks?"

"Yes. Well there's been a fair amount of reviewing cancellation marks too actually."

Susan sighed. "I don't know if I'm more shocked that you're in MI5... or that MI5 thought you were the man for the job."

"I get that a lot. It actually helps me," Ian said laughing.

"I'm not actually a member of MI5, I'm just assisting them on a few... erm... special projects."

She smiled. Just a little.

And for a moment, they sat in silence, side by side, holding hands tightly, while Max FaceTimed Daisy from the sofa and Tolstoy sniffed every inch of the room, eventually nesting on a very expensive, large scatter cushion.

Daisy was mid-transit, on her way home from Belize, flanked by two huge men in smart suits. She was furious. "What the hell is going on? I've just been dragged off the beach and herded onto a plane by these two apes. They are about to load me onto a private jet to come home... to flipping Bristol Airport."

Ian interrupted. "Just do as they ask darling. I'll explain once you get here."

"It's terribly nice here dear," added Susan helpfully.

One of Daisy's minders switched off the FaceTime – mid call.

The spa might be a safe house – or 'Safe Spa' as Ian kept calling it, but for a moment, it almost felt like a holiday.

Susan and Max seemed to be slowly coming to terms with this enforced break.

**

Griffin appeared slightly red-faced and breathing harder than he liked to admit, having trotted briskly across the rose garden in a pair of trousers two shades too tight.

"Ian," he said, wiping his brow with a perfectly pressed cotton handkerchief, "might be a good idea if you took your dog for a little... constitutional. You know. Walkies. While it's still early enough."

Ian sensed that this meant more than Griffin was actually saying and quickly put Tolstoy on a lead and walked out with Griffin into the pitch-black gardens.

Once outside Ian paused. "Are you telling me to walk the dog, or is this spy code for 'go kill someone discreetly'?"

"Let's call it a hybrid situation," Griffin replied, lowering his voice. "We've picked up a thermal shadow or two along the back hedge line. No confirmation yet, but definitely human, definitely loitering, and maybe armed. We've no K9 assets on site, and I've heard your dog has a particular flair for this kind of...erm... interaction."

Ian raised an eyebrow. "You want Tolstoy to sniff them out? He's barely been trained. His idea of tactical work is chasing squirrels."

"He'll do fine," said Griffin, reaching into his jacket and pulling out a compact semi-automatic pistol with a green laser sight and silencer. He handed it to Ian casually, like it was a bottle of mineral water. "Just in case. Standard issue. Suppressed. You know the drill."

Ian took the weapon and sighed theatrically. "There was I hoping for a hot chocolate and a back rub."

Griffin snorted.

Moments later, leash clipped to the dog and weapon firmly in hand, Ian was walking across the hotel's manicured lawns with Griffin beside him and Tolstoy straining forward like a high-powered truck.

Ian released him from the leash. "Go see," Ian said simply. This was Ian's signal to Tolstoy that this was serious.

Tolstoy, as if a switch had been flipped in his large, bristling skull, stood alert. His posture changed. Focused. Eyes narrowed. He would have saluted if he had hands.

Then he was off – a bolt of shaggy, black thunder tearing fast across the grass, nostrils flaring with purpose. Locked on hard.

As Tolstoy reached the hedgerow at the rear of the property, a rustle in the thick hawthorn was followed by a sudden eruption of motion. A figure exploded out of the undergrowth, wrapped in full military camouflage like a large bush had come to life and regretted it.

He was enormous. Hulking. Built like a Soviet tractor.

Tolstoy didn't flinch. He launched straight at him, locking his teeth into the man's forearm with the full force of an enraged war dog.

The man roared – part shock, part pain – and staggered. But, somehow, he stayed on his feet, Tolstoy now dangling from his arm like a large furry, furious suitcase.

Ian and Griffin were running now towards the ensuing mayhem.

Ian skidded to a halt, raising his pistol, heart hammering in his ears. He recognised the man immediately.

"Bear Man," Ian muttered. "Of course."

A 50-Cal professional sniper rifle all set up ready to be used at the giant's feet confirmed what Bear Man was here for. A high-end Dragunov variant, beautifully maintained. This wasn't a casual stalker. This was an attempted hit – on Ian and his family.

Tolstoy snarled, shaking his head with vicious intent. Blood flying across the grass and path. Bare bone now revealed poking from Bear Man's forearm.

Ian walked up without a word and calmly shot Bear Man point blank, straight through the forehead.

There was a crack, and the back of the man's skull exited stage left.

"Put. My. Fucking. Dog. Down," Ian growled angrily, lowering his handgun.

Bear Man collapsed like a felled redwood, dragging Tolstoy down with him. The dog released his grip with a satisfied grunt and trotted in a circle like he was doing a victory lap.

Then came a second rustle.

From twenty yards along the hedge line, another figure emerged. Slighter. Sharper. It was Hatchet Face. Again, dressed in camo, this time armed with a sidearm, eyes as dead as his expression.

Ian didn't hesitate.

"Go see," Ian snapped again.

Tolstoy didn't need a second invitation. He sprinted low and fast, ears back, fury in motion.

Hatchet Face raised his weapon, but too late.

Ian shot him once – clean through the throat – and then again through his open mouth as he gasped and he then stumbled backwards. He collapsed into the hedge with a meaty thunk, twitching once or twice before becoming very still.

"Nice work," said Griffin dryly, lowering his own weapon. "Remind me why I'm here again."

"I always need you, Griffin. For your banter. Your love. And your fine singing voice," Ian joked.

Griffin rolled his eyes. "You're insufferable sometimes. Are you ever serious?"

"Only about breakfasts," Ian replied in a very serious tone.

"Oh yeah, I've heard all about your breakfasts and I've seen the expense claims to prove it," joked Griffin.

By now, several of the MI5 agents who had travelled down to the Cotswolds with Ian's family were racing across the lawn, weapons drawn, comms crackling in their ears.

Ian gestured vaguely at the two cooling corpses. "Bit late, lads. Job's done. All we need now is a mop and a forensic pathologist. We are back off to the hotel for cocoa and chocolate biscuits."

He turned to find Tolstoy... now lapping at something.

The dog was investigating Bear Man's split skull, licking curiously at the exposed brain matter like it was pâté.

"Jesus Christ, Tolstoy!" Ian shouted. "That's evidence! Get out of there, you..."

"Well waste not, want not I guess."

The dog looked up proudly, face smeared with gore, and wagged his tail.

Ian clipped the lead back on and hauled him away. "You're a disgusting little war hero, you know that?" said Ian laughing.

He fished a couple of biscuits from his jacket pocket and passed them down to his dog. Tolstoy crunched them with blood-streaked satisfaction.

"Good lad," Ian muttered, patting his head. "You've earned your dinner. Assuming you've left any room."

As they headed back toward the golden lights of the spa, Griffin fell into step beside Ian.

"Any thoughts on what we tell Susan about just now?"

Ian didn't answer straight away. He was too busy wiping dog blood off his hand and the dog's beard with a paper napkin he had in his pocket.

He sighed. "Almost nothing. Something calming possibly. Maybe something involving Reiki and yoga."

Ian went back into the hotel and had a warm shower and got ready to go to bed. Two down, one more to go, Ian thought.

As he lay in the huge hotel bed with Susan, he held her hand, kissed her cheek and rubbed her arm gently.

"I love you Mummy," he said.

"I love you too Daddy," replied Susan, oblivious to the drama outside the hotel or the fact that two very dangerous men were now dead and being transported away in zip up body bags by large men in dark suits.

***

The next day dawned with a kind of smug golden sunlight that only the Cotswolds can conjure. A gentle mist still clung to the paddocks like an emotional support blanket, and the distant bleating of pampered sheep echoed across the hills like some sort of rustic meditation tape.

The Headhunter

After a light breakfast of heritage granola, activated almond porridge, and suspiciously smug yoghurt drizzled with lavender honey, Susan decided to commit herself fully to the spa itinerary – no holds barred.

It began with a full facial involving gold leaf, fermented Icelandic moss, and what appeared to be a consultant-level aesthetician named "Craig" who spoke only in whispers and looked like the kind of large, tall candle you'd expect to find in the Vatican.

Next came hot stone therapy with Himalayan boulders said to have been personally blessed by monks, followed by a detoxifying peat mud wrap that left Susan marinated like a stylish swamp creature. There was also a session in something called a "sound pod," where she lay in a suspended mesh cocoon while Tibetan gongs chimed and someone played whale noises through a vintage synthesiser.

By midday, she had undergone: Full lymphatic drainage via something that looked like a medieval accordion; a rose quartz chakra cleanse performed by a woman called Nova who seemed faintly translucent; and a four-hand Swedish massage by two twins who moved with a freakish, mirrored synchronicity that left Susan unable to tell where her spine ended and her soul began.

Meanwhile, Ian and Max were firmly ensconced at the hotel bar.

The bar was called *The Golden Hare* – all brushed brass fittings, velvet booths in soft sage green, and bar staff who looked like they moonlighted as violinists or baristas to the stars. It smelled faintly of rosemary smoke and citrus oils, and the cocktail list read like a novella written by someone with a degree in both poetry and distillation science. Ian and Max had started to work their way through the menu in a 'Dad time' bonding session the like of which neither of them had ever experienced.

Max, perched neatly on a low leather stool, swirled a burnt-orange negroni in a heavy-cut glass, the sort of thing that cost twelve quid before you even added the gin. Ian, not usually one for cocktails, had insisted on ordering "whatever sounds like it's on fire," and was now three-quarters through a concoction called The Summer Inferno, which came with a sprig of thyme, a smouldering cinnamon stick, and what might have been a dried rose petal.

"This tastes," Ian said slowly, blinking, "like a very angry garden centre."

Max sniffed his drink, nodded approvingly. "Yours literally came in a goblet. Is that a gold-rimmed goblet?"

"It's aspirational drinking," Ian said, swirling it like he knew what he was doing. "When in Rome – or, in this case, the Cotswolds with spa robes and an armed protection detail... do as the Cotswoldians do."

The barman, wearing a waistcoat and a knowing smirk, placed a bowl of designer almonds – dusted with something delicious – between them with the solemnity of a royal decree. Ian peered into it, grabbed one, chewed thoughtfully.

"Tastes like food of the gods," he muttered.

Max grinned. "I kind of like it here," he replied slurring slightly

Ian looked at his son, silhouetted against the mirrored back wall of the bar, where apothecary bottles glowed like stained glass in a church devoted entirely to gin. For a moment, something like peace hovered between them.

"Do you ever think," Max said, sipping, "that life's just a long series of decisions made by very drunk people in rooms like this?"

Ian nodded. "All the best decisions are."

They sat back, legs stretched out, soaking in the atmosphere. In the corner, a harpist in an embroidered jacket played a slowed-down, jazz version of Bowie's Heroes, and a waiter nearby suggested that they try the saffron and cardamom sour next.

Ian reached for a second cocktail, this one called Citrus of the Soul, which came with a tiny wooden peg clipped to the rim holding a rolled-up quote from Aristotle.

He unrolled it. It read: Happiness depends upon ourselves.

He snorted. "Depends on how good the bar staff are, more like."

Max raised his glass. "To very weird holidays."

Ian clinked his own against it. "And even weirder families."

Then Ian raised a finger. "Shh. I think I've just invented a new cocktail. I'm calling it the 'Tolstoy's Revenge.' It's gin, Angostura bitters, and the tears of a frightened bar man."

At that moment, two large men in MI5-issue smart-casual wear entered the lounge, looking crumpled and haunted – with the kind of look of men who had probably just wrestled an influencer across three continents. Between them, glaring at her phone like it had insulted her, was Daisy.

"Hello, darling," Ian called, waving his glass drunkenly in the air as if this explained everything.

Daisy did not respond. She simply strode past them and said to one of the burly men, "If you so much as breathe in my direction again, I will hack your wife's Peloton."

The larger minder looked genuinely unnerved.

But within half an hour, Daisy was in a fluffy robe with the hotel's logo embroidered on the back and was deep into her first acupuncture session while simultaneously rebranding the spa's digital presence from her iPad.

"I don't *trust* reiki," she said to her mother, needles jutting from her like a stylish porcupine. "But God, this lighting is excellent."

Susan, floating in a haze of eucalyptus mist, merely smiled. "You'll come around. You just need your chakras rebalanced."

"My chakras are fully curated, thanks," replied Daisy.

That evening, as the sun dipped behind the honeyed stone walls of the retreat, a rare thing happened.

For the first time in many, many months – perhaps even many, many years – the Taylor family relaxed.

Susan was radiant with spa serenity, Daisy had fallen asleep halfway through a Himalayan salt bath with rose petals and an audiobook of "The Power of Now," Max was considering whether or not he should train to become a cocktail mixologist (just for the lifestyle), and Ian was lying flat on a sun lounger, his belly gently falling and rising, holding a tumbler of whisky in one hand and Tolstoy's leash in the other. He was worried that Tolstoy might have got a taste for human brains – although looking at most of the minders and hotel staff maybe that wasn't actually going to be a problem at the hotel.

Before long Tolstoy was snoring. So was Ian.

Somewhere in the bushes, an armed MI5 agent in camouflage was also snoring too. Griffin would be furious if he found out, but for now, peace held all round.

The Taylors weren't safe. Not truly. Not with Duffy still out there.

But for this moment – amidst luxury robes, rosehip oils, and endless tiny sandwiches – they were, at last, a family again.

And Ian, lying there drifting in and out of consciousness, half-drunk with his trousers slightly unbuttoned, found himself actually missing the arguments over the recycling bin, the holes in his socks, the suspicious looks from neighbours, and Susan's obsession with fennel tea.

He woke briefly, smiled to himself, burped loudly, and whispered, "God, I love my life."

High above the hotel, a large lone bird of prey carved slow silent circles through the dusk. Its vast wings barely shifted, gliding on invisible currents like it owned the sky. Bronze feathers caught the last shreds of light, but there was no warmth in its gaze – only hunger and calculation. It drifted, patient, eyes fixed on the quiet grounds below. Watching. Waiting.

Chapter Eight

Don't Lose Your Head

"If the briefing makes total sense, you've probably walked into the wrong room."
~ DGSE New Agent Orientation Guide

Chapter 8

Don't Lose Your Head

Of course, this domestic idyll – the spa days, the intimate Father and Son whisky evenings, the suspiciously fluffy towels – couldn't last forever. Not when Ian Taylor had unfinished business. And unfinished business, in Ian's world, usually came with a fake passport, high powered firearms and mild concussion.

Once Griffin was confident that Susan, Max, and Daisy were safe – well-fed, fully watered, spa-soaked, and beginning to treat the security detail as glorified waiters – he and Ian agreed it was time to go hunting for Mr Duffy again.

Malcolm Duffy had been spotted - recently. Alone, this time. In Vienna.

"Vienna again?" Ian had sighed when Griffin told him. "I'm starting to get frequent flyer points with Austrian Airlines. They'll be giving me a yodelling-themed neck pillow before very long."

Griffin gave a tight smile. "We need eyes. Nothing fancy. Just watch. See if he resurfaces."

"Like a half inflated Lilo in a swimming pool," Ian muttered.

Ruth, back at Post Office HQ, was told not to expect Ian anytime soon. Griffin – never one to miss the opportunity for bureaucratic sleight of hand – had arranged for an official sick note claiming that Ian had contracted a highly contagious, deeply unpleasant, and profoundly anti-social tropical condition during his last trip to Singapore. The kind that made colleagues avert their eyes and HR departments issue confidential memos. The note was signed by a top specialist in tropical diseases at UCLH, Euston. A certain Professor G. Riffin, no less.

"Has anyone ever died from it?" Ruth had asked him over the phone with mild concern.

"Oh yes," Griffin had replied. "Several times. In multiple hemispheres. He should be fine though. He just needs time to recuperate."

Jim, meanwhile, couldn't come on this particular adventure Some minor diplomatic emergency in Malta involving a misdirected drone strike, a goat, and an ambassador's wife with a fondness for expensive designer handbags.

So, Ian flew solo.

Vienna greeted him like an immaculately dressed ex who knew exactly how good they looked and had no intention of letting him forget it. The air was cold, sharp with the threat of rain, and the cobbled streets glistened with a suspicious sort of cleanliness that suggested skullduggery at municipal level. The taxi from the airport smelled of liniment. The driver said nothing. Neither did Ian. It was the kind of peace only found between men united by mutual grumpiness and extreme lower back pain.

The hotel – the Hotel Kaiserblick – was just the right side of decadent. Marbled foyer. Crisp linen. A grand piano that played itself. The sort of place where minor royalty might discreetly get divorced.

Ian checked in under the name Gerald Stampington, admired the complimentary slippers and bathrobe, and flung himself down onto the emperor-sized bed like a weary walrus at nap time. It had been a long and difficult few months.

That evening, he treated himself to a meal at the hotel restaurant, Glanz und Gabel – a velvet-draped affair staffed by men (and women) in waistcoats.

He ordered a dry martini, then another, followed by venison with a dark cherry jus and something that involved truffles and a curious foam that added very little apart from cost.

It was magnificent.

This one was going to have to go on his MI5 expenses under "field sustenance." He couldn't charge anything to Post Office, not when he was supposed to be laying in a hospital bed, incapacitated by a rare tropical disease.

Later, in his room, he sat in silence. Vienna twinkled below the window like a snow globe powered by ambition and espresso. He checked his phone. No messages. He half-hoped Susan might have texted – something brief, something tender. She hadn't. He understood. Five Star spa treatments came before sentiment.

He fell asleep to the sound of Austrian jazz filtering through the walls and the soft gurgle of an over-engineered minibar fridge.

The next morning, someone had slid a note under his bedroom door.

A pale envelope. Plain. No hotel markings. Inside, just a single piece of card:

"I have information about where to find Mr Duffy. Meet me at Café Kleiner Morgen, 11:15am. It's in the alley off Schattengasse."

No name. No signature. Just the smell of danger written in a perfect cursive hand.

Ian read it three times. Held it to the light. Sniffed it – out of habit more than expertise.

He should've known better.

The address was too ordinary. The time too specific. And people who really had information about Malcolm Duffy didn't send handwritten notes like a Jane Austen character with an urge to tell all.

Still, curiosity's a hard itch to ignore. And so, at 11:13am, Ian stepped into the alleyway off Schattengasse to investigate further.

It was narrow. Too narrow. The kind of place where time paused and shadows lurked.

He passed an old wrought iron gate. A graffiti-smeared drainpipe. A stray cat looked at him and fled. Somewhere above, a window creaked shut… or was that open.

And then the world tipped sideways.

Thunk!

A pain to the side of his neck – sharp and sudden.

He spun, but the alley whirled. His legs crumpled. His breath fled.

There was a hand. A blur. A hiss. A voice?

Then, nothing.

Just the echo of Vienna. The drip of a distant tap. The rustle of leaves. And the cold cobbles rushing up to meet him.

***

Cold concrete. Pain. Darkness. And the sharp, sterile bite of industrial disinfectant.

Ian came to with the dull throb of a headache blooming behind his eyes and the uncomfortable awareness that his arms were strapped to a simple wooden chair with gaffer tape of some sort. His wrists ached and itched from the restraints. His legs were bound too. The room was cold – so cold it felt like the floor itself was leeching the warmth from his spine. A single bare bulb swung overhead, casting lurching shadows across the high-tech dungeon. The light buzzed with a rhythmic flicker that seemed to taunt him with every sway.

Opposite him, standing like a smug school headmaster who'd just caught someone smoking behind the bike sheds at lunchtime, was Malcolm Duffy.

Same cardigan. Same slippers. But something colder in his eyes now – not just mischief, but pure malice.

"Hello, Ian," he said pleasantly, as if they had just bumped into each other at the local garden centre.

"You've been proving to be quite a nuisance."

"You aren't the first to notice this," Ian croaked, his voice like sandpaper, mouth dry. "And I doubt you'll be the last."

"I had to dart you I am afraid, I hope you don't mind?" continued Duffy.

The lair – if one could call it that – was as minimalist as an Audi showroom. Polished concrete floors reflected the dim light like ice. The walls were seamless, as if hewn from some industrial glacier. Banks of screens lined one side, each showing feeds from different locations – most of them with thermal or night-vision overlays. High shelves housed trays of what looked like chemical compounds, wires, mechanical limbs. It was half laboratory, half modern art installation with a dash of added serial killer.

Duffy smiled, pacing like a headmaster enjoying detention a bit too much.

"You thought I collected ceramic dogs," he said, trailing his fingers over a panel. "But I collect all sorts of things. Plants. Birds. Stamps... People."

He paused beside a reinforced glass door and tapped in a code. "Let me introduce you to Ozzy. Although I believe you've already had the pleasure."

The door hissed open and in strutted an enormous bird of prey – a Golden Eagle, proud and vast, its wings rustling with regal menace. It looked like it could carry off a sheep without much bother. Its eyes were molten amber. Its talons clicked menacingly on the concrete floor.

Duffy moved beside the creature with the ease of a seasoned handler. "Ozzy," he said softly, feeding the bird a strip of something suspiciously raw.

"Beautiful, isn't he? Ozzy's more than just feathers and fury though. He's a marvel of modern technology. Tiny camera mounted on the head. Real-time streaming. And an integrated auditory cue system. I trained him with a system of clicks – different frequencies for different commands. Want him to track a scent? Click. Circle overhead? Click click. Divebomb? Well... you get the idea."

Ian stared. "You're using a tactical bird drone."

"Oh Ian," Duffy tutted. "So dismissive. He's family. And he's been watching you for months. You wouldn't believe the footage we've got. Your hotel breakfasts alone deserve their own TV series."

He clicked his fingers. The bird flew back into the shadows.

Then, with the theatrical calm of a man lighting a cigar before detonating dynamite to blow up a building, Duffy turned to the smooth concrete wall behind him. He pressed a recessed, brushed steel button – something you'd expect to find controlling the mood lighting in an upscale Berlin hotel. The wall responded with a soft hydraulic sigh, splitting horizontally with clinical precision before gliding open.

What it revealed was not mood lighting. It was madness, codified.

Behind the panel lay a long, recessed chamber, perhaps ten feet across and softly backlit – part museum exhibit, part mausoleum. The air felt colder, damper. As if something had breathed its last here and never quite left.

Mounted on blackened oak plinths were the preserved heads of at least two dozen individuals – arranged in perfect rows, each with a uniform brass nameplate gleaming beneath them. They weren't crude. They weren't rotting. These had been expertly embalmed, carefully preserved. Some with faint make-up, others with glass eyes so lifelike they seemed to watch Ian as he stared back at them.

He recognised some of the faces.

To the left: Brigadier Charles Dunley, MI5 – stiff upper lip even in death, moustache waxed to a defiant curl. Plate read: *"Poisoned. Bruges. 2008."*

Next to him: Simone Vachelle, formerly of the DGSE – her lips caught forever in a soft 'oh', as if her final breath had been a mid-rebuke. *"Thrown from train. Montreux. 2013."*

Oren Wolf, Mossad – half his lower jaw missing, but the fire somehow still smouldering in his one good eye. *"Sniper. Tbilisi. 2018."*

Agent Theodore "Tank" Reynolds, CIA – his head so broad it required custom mounting brackets. Teeth bared, possibly in laughter, possibly in fury. *"Throat slit. Marrakesh. 2011."*

There was a head encased in a partial deep-sea diving helmet. Another adorned with a garland of digital watch faces – each stopped at the exact time of death. Some were bald. Some had dyed hair. One wore a pince-nez. One still had an earpiece with the wire trailing like a question mark.

Interpol. NATO. Even a North Korean defector, still with his medal bar pinned to a remnant of uniform, like a joke only Duffy found funny.

Each face was frozen in time. Some surprised. Some stoic. Some heartbreakingly peaceful, like they'd finally let go. The room had the feel of a twisted gallery, or the world's worst after-dinner speakers' panel.

And in the centre, framed with a brass trim and spotlighted with theatrical precision, was a conspicuously empty space. A velvet-lined mount waited. No head. Just a place reserved.

Above it: a plaque already etched in immaculate serif lettering:

Ian Taylor
"Post Office Man. Shambling Buffoon. Crack Assassin."

Duffy stepped to it with quiet reverence. His voice dropped to something near a prayer.

"That's for you," he said. "The crown jewel if you will. You've lasted longer than the rest. Sloppier, yes. Hungrier, definitely. But you're not without a particular ruthless capability."

Ian didn't speak. He couldn't. His mouth had gone completely dry now, his hands damp. The sight chilled him more than the deaths themselves – because Duffy hadn't just killed these people. He had *curated* them.

A collection not of trophies, but of undone legacies. Of lives unthreaded.

And somewhere beneath his panic, a small part of Ian's brain thought:

I've got to get out of here. Now.

Ian blinked. "You've got something on your jumper. Bit of... evil. Right there on the collar."

Duffy chuckled. "Still with the jokes Ian. I like that."

"You've been watching too many James Bond movies", said Ian. "Or is that more Austin Powers?"

"You can try to insult me all you like Ian. It won't help you."

Ian grimaced. "Where's the tea, Malcolm? I thought you were supposed to be civilised."

Duffy gestured to a tray on a side table. A chipped mug, a doily underneath, and a steaming pot. "Oh, there's tea. But I'm afraid it's poisoned."

Ian discretely tested the restraints. Tensed his fingers. Stretching the tape a little – bit by bit. Making some room to manoeuvre. Then…at a stretch… he could feel it – the familiar ridge of his Post Office fob, concealed in his pocket. Inside it, hidden, a single-use flash charge. Loaded, just enough to blow a lock. Smash a chair. And possibly blow his legs right off too. But needs must.

"You know," Ian said slowly, "I always suspected your begonias were hiding something."

"Oh, Ian," Duffy sighed. "So naïve. So… provincial."

Ian, bored now, triggered the fob.

A high-pitched whine. Then a flash. A bang. Searing white light. Screaming. (Mostly Ian.)

Smoke filled the chamber like conjured mist. Ian flew backward with the force, his chair shattering into shards of splintered wood. Pain bloomed across his side. But he was free.

The smoke cleared. Ozzy dead. A pile of smoking feathers.

Duffy? Gone. Bloody typical.

Ian staggered to his feet, blinking through smoke and debris. Alarms shrieked in various registers. Sprinklers coughed to life, spitting in confused, ineffectual bursts.

Red warning lights stuttered overhead, flickering like guilty consciences.

He bolted through a side door, each step a new episode in pain. His ribs sang, his legs burned, and he was fairly certain his beard had caught fire. He slammed a fire alarm with the flat of his hand as he passed – just for good measure.

Behind him, the building let out a groan like a wounded god. Something inside exploded with a stomach-turning roar. The ceiling coughed out flames. Glass shattered. Sirens wailed in the distance.

Ian didn't look back he just moved quickly – getting out of danger. Away from Duffy. Duffy had slipped from Ian's grasp again. But the game wasn't over.

Not yet. Not by a long way.

He had work to do. Duffy was still out there.

***

Once back at his hotel, Ian showered, scrubbed char from his skin, and patched up his legs with an alarming amount of hotel mini-Elastoplast. He dressed in the least-flammable clothing he could find – beige cargo trousers and a linen shirt two sizes too big – and checked out looking like a man who had either just escaped a hostage situation or accidentally joined a curious cult – where they worshiped Elastoplast.

Ian took a cab to the airport and got the first flight he could back to Heathrow,

At Heathrow, Jim and Griffin collected him in a nondescript government-issued black Volvo with tinted windows and a glove box full of high-powered weapons and protein bars. Ian grunted a greeting and fell asleep before they had even left the car park. He was exhausted.

Several hours later, they rolled up to the Cotswold spa hotel hideaway, Ian looking like a returning monarch being smuggled home from exile.

Susan, Max and Daisy were on the sun-drenched terrace sipping herbal tea and nibbling on lavender shortbread.

Ian emerged from the car like a man who had been lightly grilled, then reheated. Tolstoy barked and launched himself at Ian, knocking over a garden lounger and a member of staff carrying iced towels.

"You look like a burnt kebab that's been dropped on the Tube," said Susan, inspecting her husband with the critical eye of someone who had just won a bet.

"Thank you, my darling. It's good to see you too."

***

Over the next few days, Ian did his best to recuperate. By which, of course, meant overeat, over-soak, over-gossip, and generally undermine the entire concept of mindfulness.

He booked himself in for just about every treatment available on the spa menu. Hot stone massage ("It's like being paved for a luxury patio!"), reflexology ("Is it supposed to feel like someone's adjusting the gears on a vintage bicycle inside your feet?"), and a reiki session during which he snored so loudly the therapist gave up and had a nap herself.

He was banned from the cryo-chamber after insisting it was "a test of true masculinity" and attempting to race a member of the hotel staff in just his underpants. The mud wrap treatment ended prematurely when Ian mistook the mud pack left on his tray for a healthy chocolate spa snack and began spreading it on his oatcakes.

"I thought it was artisan hummus," he grumbled when confronted.

He was politely asked not to enter the ladies-only flotation pod room "ever again," and an official complaint was lodged after he was found attempting to cook a sausage roll on the aromatherapy diffuser in the eucalyptus steam room.

Meanwhile, Max and Ian bonded over cocktails in the snug bar. Max drank just every option on the menu. And Ian ordered anything with an umbrella or fire hazard attached and regaled his son with completely made-up stories of Cold War philatelists and stamp-themed near-death experiences.

Susan and Daisy eased themselves into a routine of massages, reading in hammocks, and stopping Ian from eating the potpourri. Susan tolerated his antics with an eyeroll and the occasional death glare, particularly after he attempted to "improve" the hydrotherapy circuit by setting off the hot tub jets manually and bellowing "ACTIVATE TRIPWIRES" while standing on a water feature.

The spa staff were on the verge of gently, firmly escorting him from the premises. It was only Susan's intervention – delivered with a tilt of the head and a smile like an unsheathed blade – that saved him.

"If you get yourself killed mucking about, Ian Taylor," she warned, "I won't remarry. I'll just dance."

Ian took the hint. Briefly.

**

And then, one golden morning, Griffin arrived at the breakfast table holding a cup of black coffee and wearing his "I have news but refuse to make a fuss" expression.

He waited until the waiter had gone.

"Well?" said Ian, brushing croissant flakes from his towelling robe.

Griffin gave a small nod. "You're cleared. It's safe. Duffy's off the radar. We're putting a wrap on this one. For now."

Susan looked up from her fresh fruit and miso-tinted grapefruit. "Does that mean we can go home?"

"Yes," said Griffin, smiling. "Back to normal. Or whatever passes for that in your household."

There was a moment of quiet, broken only by the sound of Tolstoy licking yoghurt off a patio chair.

Ian smiled. He drank his tea. "Right. Let's pack."

And as the sun rose over the gentle Cotswold hills, casting light on chamomile lawns and cold-press juicers, the Taylors prepared to return to London.

Home. Chaos. Curry. And, possibly, a little danger.

But for now?

Just peace, and a man (and his dog) with mild digestive issues.

Chapter Nine
All Good Things Come to an End

"Appear gormless. Act innocently. Keep your expenses up to date."
~ MI5 Basic Fieldcraft Guide (reprinted 1989, pulped 1998)

Chapter 9

All Good Things Come to an End

Back home in North London, helped by their 'holiday', the Taylor household had slipped into something dangerously close to domestic harmony. Tolstoy lazed in patches of sun like a retired aristocrat, only occasionally lifting his head to fart or bark at a passing squirrel. Ian took him for long, meandering walks around their particular corner of north London suburban bliss, nodding at neighbours he barely recognised and buying the occasional overpriced sourdough loaf to 'fit in' and maintain appearances.

Susan had entered what Ian privately referred to as her "earth goddess phase." She was decanting lentils into mason jars with the solemnity of an apothecary, humming something vaguely Celtic while wafts of joss sticks and avocado-based optimism curled through the air. She spoke of gut health now. A lot.

Ian, to his mild astonishment, felt something like peace. His family – even Daisy – seemed to accept him. Or at least tolerate him in a less sarcastic way than usual.

"I still can't believe you're *some* sort of spy," Daisy had said, perched on the sofa with a herbal tea and an eyebrow arched high enough to interfere with satellites. "What do you even do? Email newsletters to MI6? Organise the MI5 Christmas party?"

"Yes," Ian replied flatly. "That sort of thing. Boring stuff. Risk assessments. A lot of paperwork."

Susan didn't say anything. But Ian had caught her staring at him over the top of her kombucha, a look that said: *I know you're lying. I just haven't decided if I care enough to call you out on it yet.*

Eventually, as all good things must, the bubble of calm burst under the sharp pinprick of obligation. Ian knew he couldn't put it off any longer. The Post Office wouldn't run itself. And someone, somewhere, was probably preparing to launch a disastrous commemorative stamp issue featuring an unfortunate member of the Royal Family. Duty called.

He rose early, dressed in something that smelled like it had been left in a suitcase since Geneva, and caught the 8.08 to King's Cross. The train was as packed and miserable as ever – a human terrarium of doomscrolling and bitter BO. Ian felt a peculiar comfort in its exactness.

From King's Cross he ambled along Pentonville Road, up toward Farringdon and Holborn, where the grand monolith of Post Office HQ loomed like a disapproving mother, waiting for him to get home late after playing at the park after dark.

The Headhunter

The air smelt of diesel, wet pavement and bureaucracy.

Nobody welcomed him back. Or even particularly acknowledged him.

Not a card. Not a gift. Not a banner. No balloons with his name on. Not even a smile. It was as if he'd simply stepped out for a long lunch.

Ian entered the lift with the dead-eyed stare of a man going to his own funeral. The doors pinged shut. Smooth jazz Muzak played. He hated being back already.

Up on the first floor, he found a desk – exactly as he'd left it. Slightly wonky. With a packet of half-finished biscuits, he had bought – and half finished – before he had left, before his impromptu 'holiday'.

He logged in.

17,569 emails were waiting for him.

He stared at the screen. Blinked. Then selected them all and deleted the lot in one fell swoop.

"If it's important," he muttered, "they'll email again."

He leaned back and took in the dull, comforting glow of pointless spreadsheets and outdated intranet pages. No danger. No poison. No golden eagles. No Malcolm Duffy. Just run of the mill corporate tedium. It was oddly cathartic.

That serenity lasted less than three minutes.

He heard the click of expensive heels and the chirpy clatter of someone trying far too hard to seem normal.

Ruth.

"Ian! Oh, it's sooo good to see you back," she chirped, her voice drenched in HR sincerity. "How do you feel? Are you –" and here she paused dramatically, " – fully cured... erm recovered I mean?"

Ian spun around slowly in his chair, briefly contemplating the idea of faking a post-traumatic stammer or claiming he now only spoke in Latin.

"I'm feeling much better, thank you, Ruth. Strong. Resilient. Dangerously capable of returning to inbox-based duties."

"That's *wonderful*," she said, as if she'd personally healed him with a LinkedIn post. "Because there are going to be some more changes around here, I am afraid. I'm, erm, well pregnant...um expecting a baby."

"Congratulations," Ian replied. "How marvellous. All the best to you and... your co-producer."

"Yes, and I'll be going on maternity leave very soon. And you'll have a new line manager – Sebastian. Erm Seb. South African. Very nice man."

Ian winced. His past experiences with men described as "very nice" and "South African" in the same sentence usually ended with him being shouted at and, more often than not, body shamed.

"And!" Ruth continued, with the self-satisfaction of someone delivering terrible news wrapped in a congratulatory ribbon, "We're taking you off philatelic products. Too much pressure for one person. Plus... the expenses. Good God!"

"The breakfasts?" Ruth continued, in a slightly strained, high-pitched voice.

"Five Olympic breakfasts in one day. *Two days running*, Ian. And the piano incident. We had to pay to have it restrung. And the flatulence in front of the Swiss ambassador. The CEO received a *letter*."

"His wife laughed," Ian said defensively.

"She was crying," Ruth replied abruptly. Anyway, we're moving you to Corporate Transformation Comms. Potential for more home working. Fewer grand pianos. Less reputational risk all round."

Ian nodded slowly.

He didn't care. He couldn't face another commemorative butterfly stamp or royal wedding envelope snafu anyway.

Besides, transformation sounded vaguely heroic. He could live with that.

"Anyway, welcome back," Ruth said with manufactured warmth. "Try not to cause any further international incidents."

"No promises," Ian said cheerfully.

He turned back to his screen. A new email had just landed in his inbox – marked 'Urgent and highly confidential' It was titled:

"Keeping your Office Lanyards secure when you are away from the office."

He smiled.

It was good to be back – to the acres of grey carpets, seating pods, banks of unmanned workstations, online training modules and spreadsheets.

Ian's secure phone gave a soft but urgent ping.

Ian didn't even blink. Without ceremony, he stood up from his desk, muttered something about an urgent meeting in room G-1749 to no one in particular, and made a beeline for the Post Office's third-floor toilets – also known, in certain circles, as Ian's MI5 emergency satellite office.

He locked himself into the furthest cubicle, the one with the broken coat hook and the mysterious ceiling stain. Out came the 'secret' encrypted phone from his inner jacket pocket.

GRIFFIN:
WE'VE PICKED UP THE TRAIL. DUFFY IS IN ARGENTINA. SEE YOU AT THE LAUNDERETTE. 15:00.

Ian stared at the words. His stomach gave a little jolt – not quite fear, not quite excitement. Something between the two. 'Dreadjoy' seemed somehow appropriate.

Here we go again, he thought, tucking the phone away and unlocking the cubicle door. His first thought, as ever in a time of crisis, was simple:

"I need another breakfast."

Hobbits have second breakfasts Ian mused. And hobbits rarely had to fight psychopathic philatelists in remote South American hideaways. Ian reckoned he deserved at least two pastries and a sausage sandwich and perhaps a little scrambled egg.

At 14:59, Ian pushed open the fogged glass door of the launderette, the doorbell jingling like a nervous tambourine. It was, as ever, a temple of low-budget despair. Machines clunked and sighed like they were slowly dying of ennui. A single sock clung to the inside of a dryer window like a warning from a parallel universe.

Griffin was already there, folding something suspiciously like military-grade sheets with the precision of a man who had never, not once in his life, used a fitted one.

"You look well," Ian said.

"You look like you've been left out in the rain with the bins," Griffin replied, not looking up. "But never mind that. We've found him. Duffy."

"Let me guess – somewhere easy and relaxing, like Burnley?"

"Argentina. Patagonian border. He's set himself up in a secluded compound by a river tributary. Remote. Heavily surveilled. Drones in the sky. Satellite blind spots. The usual."

Ian sighed. "Any more signs of eagles?"

"Unknown. But if you see any more, try not to make eye contact. We've had letters from the RSPB since you blew up that Golden Eagle in Vienna."

Griffin handed him a thick manila file. It smelled of printer toner and envelope gum.

"You'll be going in ten days. With Jim. This time we end it once and for all."

Ian nodded, serious now. "And Susan? The kids? Are they safe?"

"Still safe. We've enhanced surveillance on the house, added a few extra layers of security. They'll be fine."

"Good," said Ian, sliding the file into his battered leather briefcase. "I'm not going through all this just to come home to find the house in ruins with Tolstoy running the place."

Ian decided to go and check out his luxury penthouse deep in the City. He hadn't been there for weeks and wanted to check it was all OK.

***

His penthouse – a minimalist symphony of utter luxury, polished steel, smart glass, and flooring so perfect it may have been created from star dust and magic. The apartment was immaculate, perfectly maintained and cleaned to within an inch of its life by his MI5 paymasters. He needn't have worried.

Ian sprawled on the smart designer sofa with a 25-year-old whisky and opened the file Griffin had handed him at the launderette.

Photographs. Satellite imagery. Floor plans. Travel manifests. It was all there.

The photographs showed that Duffy's compound was vast. A Bavarian style mansion tucked into a bend on a remote river, flanked by thick forest and a drone net that ran daily patrols like clockwork. There were security cameras, motion sensors, even rumoured EM field disruption equipment. There was a sea plane to enable Duffy to easily get in and out easily too.

And rumours of more very large, trained birds of prey.

Ian rubbed his temples. "If I get taken out by an Andean condor with a GoPro strapped to its head, I'm going to be livid."

He checked his work email again on his work laptop to see if any new emails had arrived. Sitting there, waiting for him, was a blunt and punctuation-deficient message from HR – glaring up at him. It had just arrived in his inbox.

** FROM: Corporate Travel & Ethics
SUBJECT: EXPENSES – URGENT
Dear Ian,
After a recent audit of your expenses and certain regrettable incidents involving multiple, extravagant Swiss

breakfasts, dry cleaning for senior diplomats, a damaged piano and a broken fondue set, your corporate card is suspended. No further claims will be reimbursed. Please destroy your Post Office Corporate Card and return it to us at Head Office reception. **

Regards,
Janine
Corporate Ethics Administrator

Ian closed the email and gave the screen a slow, deliberate middle finger to the computer screen.

No matter. Griffin's budgets were unofficial, unlimited, and MI5 was blissfully disinterested in things like receipts or episodes where pianos were ruined – in fact they half encouraged it.

When he eventually arrived home that night only Tolstoy was there. Susan, Max and Daisy had all gone to the cinema to watch a film they had all wanted to see for ages about an International Assassin. Ian wasn't all that keen – unsurprisingly.

Susan had left a note.

"We have all gone to the cinema. Don't worry two of Griffins' men have gone with us. Shepherds Pie is in the fridge.

He poured himself a further whisky, this time supermarket own label, and dropped onto the sofa, and muttered to Tolstoy – who was snoring contentedly on a rug made of antimicrobial yak fleece:

"Well, boy. I'm going to miss you while I'm away."

Tolstoy sighed contentedly in reply, without opening his

eyes.

Ian raised his glass of amber liquid and gave the dog a solemn nod.

"To Argentina," he said, "and to finishing what I bloody well started."

Tolstoy yawned, unimpressed.

***

It was 06:23 a.m. when Ian and Jim arrived at Heathrow Airport – Terminal 5. Ian was dressed like a home surveyor having a midlife crisis: chinos too tight, blazer too loud, sunglasses already on indoors. Jim wore a muted travel outfit and the air of a man who deeply regretted every international trip with Ian since the Cold War.

They stood at the check-in desk, First Class queue, flanked by two large, battered suitcases and a cardboard box with "ESSENTIAL EQUIPMENT – DO NOT SHAKE" scrawled across it. Inside: an inflatable camping bed, an inflatable kayak, and what Ian insisted was a "highly personalised picnic set."

"I can't believe you even brought some of Tolstoy's biscuits," Jim muttered.

"You never know," said Ian. "Might need to bribe a border guard dog. Anyway, they are delicious and full of iron. They could be the difference between starvation and survival."

The BA check-in staff, faced with Ian's passport (slightly burnt at one corner and damp at the spine) and Jim's travel credentials, looked as though they'd rather be serving jet fuel Frappuccino's in the Costa downstairs.

"Do you have anything to declare?" the woman asked politely.

"Yes," Ian said. "I declare this shirt to be a cultural artefact. And, also, that your boarding pass design is fundamentally uninspiring."

Jim coughed loudly in protest. "Let's try to keep things low profile," he said quietly.

To no, or little, avail.

They made it through security with minimal incidents – though Ian's belt did set off a metal detector, and he had loudly debated with the members of Customs staff whether the body scanner might give him superpowers.

***

The Concord Room was, as always, a temple of quiet luxury. Plush armchairs, oak panelling, and soft jazz playing through a sound system that whispered, "don't ever mention economy class or pre-prepared meals."

Ian was in heaven. And havoc.

Within minutes he had:

Spilled a bottle of champagne into a vase of orchids.

Requested four full English breakfasts from the waiter and asked the sommelier which wine best paired with a bacon sandwich.

Sneaked some of Tolstoy's favourite dog chews into the glass display of macarons – just to confuse other travellers.

He also attempted to operate the espresso machine and instead flooded the juice bar with coffee.

Jim, sipping a strong black coffee and pretending not to know him, sighed. Loudly.

"You realise," Jim said, "that MI5 doesn't actually cover the damages?"

"Rubbish," Ian replied. "This is diplomatic soft power. I'm showing the world British greatness. Through the medium of unlimited hash browns and the power of incompetence and chaos."

"I'm going to get another croissant," Jim said, standing up. "When I come back, I want you to be in the same chair, not trying to hotwire the massage chair again."

"It winked at me," Ian said defensively. "I thought it wanted to be friends."

By 09:00, Ian had moved on to the Bloody Mary bar and was onto his second attempt to build what he called "The Tower of London" – a cocktail stacked with celery, olives, bacon rashers, and a boiled egg.

"Think I'll need a lie-down on the plane," he muttered, eyes beginning to glaze. "Also, I've eaten seventeen pigs-in-blankets. That's a personal best."

Jim returned from a trip to the toilet just in time to see Ian attempting to mix gin with what he thought was tomato juice, but which turned out to be beetroot gazpacho.

"I hope Argentina has hospitals," Jim said.

"I hope Argentina has more of this goat's cheese," said Ian, mouth full. "Because I've just stuffed most of it into my pockets for the flight - rations."

***

As the first-class announcement rang out for the flight from Gate B12, Ian stood tall – or wobbly, depending on how you looked at it – and pulled on his face mask. His jacket now bulged suspiciously with stolen cured meats and other foodstuffs.

"You realise we're flying into the middle of a jungle war zone?" Jim asked as they joined the short boarding queue.

"Exactly," Ian grinned. "Which is why I'm loading up on sliced meats, cheese and smoked trout. Field survival, Jim. It's all about preparation."

They took their seats – flat beds, cashmere blankets monogrammed with tiny crowns – and Ian immediately requested a warm flannel, two gin tonics, and a pencil to doodle a rudimentary escape plan on his napkin.

"Here we go again," said Jim, settling in with a sigh.

"To Patagonia," said Ian, raising his glass. "And to ending this once and for all."

"And to the poor sod who has to sit next to you," Jim muttered.

Ian leaned back, looked at the clouds outside, and smiled.

"Jim?"

"Yes?"

"If I die on this mission, make sure Tolstoy gets my cufflinks."

Jim nodded solemnly.

They clinked glasses as the plane lifted off the tarmac, soaring into a future that almost certainly involved danger, deception… and possibly a further breakfast.

Chapter Ten
The Long Shot

"Disguise begins with silence. And sometimes with borrowed trousers."
~ **Internal training memo, Mossad (Code: HUSH-71)**

Chapter 10

The Long Shot

When they landed in Argentina it was early morning. Jim and Ian were both very jet lagged and full of endless breakfasts and far too many gin and tonics.

The Buenos Aires arrivals terminal was a blur of humidity, stern-looking customs agents, and the scent of duty-free cologne. As Ian and Jim emerged into the thick heat of Argentina's summer, they were immediately flanked by three hulking operatives from the local MI5 field office. Each of them looked like they could bench press a Renault Clio.

"Welcome to South America, gentlemen," the leader said. His name was Diego, his voice gravelly and unbothered by vowels. "We have weapons and transport waiting. Please follow us."

"In that order?" Ian muttered. "Because I'd quite like a beer first."

Jim elbowed him gently. "Let the nice assassins do their job."

The SUV they were bundled into was black, matte, and made of angles. In the back, under a heavy tarpaulin, sat a small armoury that would've made NATO blink.

"We've got M4 carbines, Sig Sauer P226s, two Franchi SPAS-12 shotguns, a Barratt 50-Cal, a pair of suppressed MP5Ks, tactical knives, flashbangs, thermal goggles, and a collapsible rocket launcher," Diego announced, barely glancing at the contents.

"Oooh," Ian cooed, holding up a thermal scope like a child at Christmas. "Do we get to keep these?"

"Only if you survive," Diego replied, utterly deadpan.

Their journey took them through increasingly winding mountain roads until they reached a glittering blue lake that shimmered with mountain runoff and mosquito larvae the size of tortellini. Parked by a crude jetty was a twin-engine seaplane that looked like it had last passed inspection when Ronald Regan was US President.

"Please tell me that's just for show," Ian said, eyeing the rusting float pontoons and the duct tape holding one wing strut together.

"She'll get us there," said Diego, with the optimism of a man who had clearly never been in the air with Ian before.

The pilot introduced only as "Gato," lit a cigarette with a look that said he'd seen some things. Possibly from the air. Possibly while the plane was on fire.

Jim climbed aboard, grimacing at the smell of petrol, sat down on a hard seat, which exhaled air. "I think my seat just screamed," he said.

"Probably haunted," Ian added.

"Probably a warning," said Jim.

The flight to Patagonia was long, low, and loud. The seaplane juddered through updrafts with the enthusiasm of a shopping trolley on cobbles. Through the windows, the scenery changed from lush green to wild mountain crags, until finally they descended over a network of river tributaries that glittered like broken glass under the afternoon sun.

They landed with a teeth-rattling splash somewhere along the Rio Pico, their pontoons skimming the water like stones on a Scottish loch. The plane glided toward a makeshift jetty cobbled together from oil drums and old rope, where the other two local operatives had already set up a small camp.

It consisted of three tents, a portable satellite dish, a folding table covered in ammunition and energy drinks, and a small generator that sputtered like an asthmatic chainsaw.

Ian immediately clocked the pile of food supplies.

"Do I see... chorizo?" he asked, bounding over and unzipping one of the coolers. "My God, Jim. They brought Manchego. This may be the most civilised jungle base I've ever seen."

"You've only seen one once before," Jim replied, swatting a mosquito the size of a sparrow. "And we were very nearly eaten by a Komodo Dragon that time."

Still, Ian busied himself assembling a sandwich so structurally elaborate it required planning permission and engineering approval. Around them, the mosquitoes came in waves, laughing at repellent and targeting English skin like it was a gourmet banquet.

"Why are they ignoring you?" Ian hissed at Diego, who stood completely unbothered.

"Local blood," Diego said. "They know not to mess with me."

Jim batted another mosquito away from his eyelid. "They're trying to take my watch."

"Get used to it," Diego said. "Welcome to the jungle."

As night fell, the group lit a perimeter of citronella torches and dug into their rations. Ian spent an inordinate amount of time selecting cheeses.

"So, what's the plan?" he eventually asked, wiping grease from his chin with a map.

"Tomorrow," Diego said, "we move upriver. Duffy's compound is heavily fortified. He's got thermal drones on 24-hour cycles, motion sensors, guard towers, and probably a small army of ethically murky mercenaries."

"Sounds just the way we like to party," Jim muttered.

"Can we assume some of Duffy's eagles might be in play again?" Ian asked, casually slicing salami.

"Possibly. But we've packed anti-avian countermeasures for them."

Ian raised an eyebrow. "Do those come in the form of rocket launchers?"

"Actually," Diego said, "yes."

Ian smiled with real warmth. "I think I'm going to like this mission."

The fire crackled. The insects buzzed. And somewhere far upriver, in a compound bristling with surveillance, Malcolm Duffy stared at a monitor, watching the faint blip of a seaplane land. His eyes narrowed. A smile played on his lips.

"Welcome back, Mr Taylor," he whispered to the screen.

***

Ian woke with a jolt, heart racing and sleeping bag wet with sweat. His nightmare had been horrifically vivid – Duffy's lair, that cursed trophy wall, and the grotesque sight of Susan, Max, and Daisy's heads mounted alongside all the others. He'd screamed himself awake. Jim sleeping like an oversized cushion at the end of the cot, blinked once and promptly went back to sleep with a flatulent sigh.

It was five a.m.

By six, the whole camp was awake, dragged out of their hammocks and into strategy talk by Ian, who paced in over tight combat trousers, with a mosquito-bitten neck, looking somewhat like a demented scoutmaster.

"Look," Ian began, waving a half-eaten bacon sandwich, "Duffy's clever – diabolically clever. He probably already knows we're here. Hell, he probably sent someone over the river to poison my cheese stash during the night."

Jim, bleary-eyed and brushing his teeth with cold coffee, nodded. "Would explain the dreams you were having. You kept shouting something about beheadings and dismemberment."

"I suggest we send a decoy," Ian continued, unbothered. "Someone who looks like me. Lumbers like me. Distracts like me. Meanwhile, Jim and I sneak through the jungle, get set up with this monster." He thumped the black case containing the Barrett .50 calibre sniper rifle. "And when Duffy steps into the open, we blow the smug right out of him."

A moment of silence.

"Who in this group is going to pretend to be you?" asked one of the Argentine operatives, looking doubtful.

Everyone turned to Diago.

"I hate all of you," muttered Diago as he was promptly stuffed into a makeshift, jerry built, handmade pillow-padded bodysuit, draped in netting, and handed a fake pair of specs to complete the Ian look.

It was surprisingly very convincing.

Two hours later, Diago readied the inflatable dingy with two other agents, getting ready to set off up-river in sight of Duffy's cameras and his many other surveillance devices.

"Just hold on here for a couple more hours," Ian asked the team by the inflatable boat. "Give Jim and I time to get set up in a good position opposite Duffy's mansion."

Jim and Ian melted into the jungle, machetes in hand. The huge rifle slung over Ian's shoulder. Jim carrying the ammunition and a bipod for the rifle.

"Map and compass," Jim grunted, pointing ahead. "Half a click uphill, then we cut across and reach the ridge. No drama."

"Which always means... lots of pain, lots of drama," muttered Ian.

It was a brutal slog lasting almost the full two hours they had available. The terrain was thick, clawing. Every plant seemed designed to slap or stab. Masses of the huge mosquitos followed like an angry Greek chorus. But eventually, panting and scratched, they reached a suitable outcrop directly opposite Duffy's fortress.

The Headhunter

It was both monstrous and beautiful, like a beautiful Bavarian mansion that would be more at home in the Black Forest region. Solar panels glinted from the rooftop. Automated drones buzzed in slow, ominous circuits high in the sky.

Jim unfolded the bipod for the Barrett rifle and set it up expertly and quickly. "This thing's really meant for armoured vehicles," he said, with reverent awe. "You sure you don't want me to do the honours?"

"No," said Ian. "This one's personal."

The sniper rifle settled into his shoulder like an eager lover. Ian peered through the scope. The crosshairs covered Duffy's front door, his sweeping front lawn, the jetty, the whole front perimeter. Ian could see it all with ease. They were in an excellent position.

Then came the carefully prepared bait.

The dingy, piloted by Diago-as-Ian, came puttering up to the landing strip, against the strong flow of the river. A moment passed. Then the boat dropped back a bit down river and then powered up to go past Duffy's house.

Then all hell broke loose.

An explosion lit up the water, lifting the dingy like paper in a hurricane high into the air. Flames. Screams. Limbs everywhere.

"Bloody hell," Ian gasped, recoiling. "He's not just prepared. He's declared war."

Jim grabbed Ian's arm. "Steady. Don't break cover. Stay still."

And then... Duffy.

He just strolled out of the house like a man out inspecting his roses, crisp white linen shirt billowing. He jogged with a smile down to the jetty and stepped into a small, sleek black speedboat, started the engine and moved towards the wreckage. His head bobbed in and out of the sniper's view like a stubborn whack-a-mole.

Ian held his breath.

Crosshairs locked. Then... movement. But not where Ian or Jim expected it.

Something low and fast shot from the treeline to their left.

"Bird incoming!" Jim shouted, pistol out.

It was enormous – another huge golden eagle with a leather-strapped camera glinting on its back. It screamed as it swooped towards them, talons extended – razor sharp.

Distracted momentarily. Ian now focused. The crosshairs now floated across Duffy's back.

Jim fired twice at the bird.

The eagle crumpled mid-air, crashing into the underbrush like a sack of wings and bones.

But Duffy had seen the muzzle flash and sensed a disturbance. He realised something was wrong and started to move quickly.

Too late.

Ian squeezed.

The recoil nearly dislocated Ian's shoulder. The echo rolled across the river.

Duffy's body convulsed and flew sideways off the boat, into the river, like a puppet having its strings cut.

There was silence.

The river rolled on, stained and indifferent.

"I think...I think... that's it," Ian said, exhaling slowly.

Jim scanned the treeline. "Did we get him?"

Ian nodded. "If we didn't, he's got a new orifice the size of a kitchen cupboard in his back, and he's learnt to breathe underwater."

They sat there in the mud, spent. Sweat-drenched. Alive.

"Let's go home, mate," said Ian.

Jim sighed. "Thank God. I'm sick of insects, humidity, the jungle and pretending I don't mind your snoring."

Ian chuckled.

"Come on," he said. "Time to go home – fortunately with our heads still attached to our bodies."

Chapter Eleven

Outside, a Barn Owl Hooted

"Silencers don't silence. They just ask politely."
~ Sniper School Graffiti, Unknown NATO Facility, Latvia

Chapter 11
Outside, a Barn Owl Hooted

Ian and Jim couldn't wait to get home. Two weeks in the jungle had left them battered, bug-bitten, and smelling of Jungle Formula, cordite and river slime. So much so that even the allure of Buenos Aires couldn't keep them for long. Still, they allowed themselves one night – just one – to rest, recuperate... and to feast.

They found a small, atmospheric parrilla near San Telmo called El Infierno del Asado. Roughly translated: The Hell of Barbecue. A fitting name, Ian thought, given the slow-roasting chaos they'd just endured in the jungle.

The interior was smoke-stained and rich with the scent of charcoal and sizzling fat. Cows in various states of glory rotated slowly on open spits. The owner, a barrel-chested man named Rodrigo with the voice of a carnival barker and the moustache of a 19th-century villain, welcomed them with a theatrical flourish.

"Carnes infinitas!" he announced. "Eat until you see God!"

"I see meat sweats in my future," Ian said.

They were given a small table by the grill, where Rodrigo kept delivering mountains of beef ribs, short rib, chorizo, blood sausage, sirloin, and something labelled only as "beef mystery."

"This one tastes like one of Tolstoys chews," Ian said, chewing thoughtfully. "But in a good way."

"Shut up and eat," said Jim, halfway through a steak the size of a small family car.

Rodrigo began to hover nervously after the third round of refills.

"Señores... are you professionals? You have bottomless stomachs. You are like military goats."

"You don't know the half of it," Jim grunted.

They shuffled back to their hotel, fell into their beds, and snored like freight trains until morning. During the night, Ian had a mild meat-induced hallucination involving Winston Churchill and a cow in a bikini. He woke in a lather and could only manage a strong coffee and some toast for breakfast.

Before boarding the flight home, Ian messaged Griffin:

ALL DONE. DUFFY SHOT WITH 50-CAL. COULDN'T FIND HIS BODY. SWEPT AWAY BY RIVER.

Griffin replied:

WELL, HE'D DO WELL TO SURVIVE A PIECE OF LEAD THAT SIZE AND A FAST PATAGONIAN CURRENT.

Feeling a lot better now, Ian switched off the phone, leaned back into his First Class seat, and ordered champagne before take-off.

He breathed a huge sign of relief and braced himself for the four meals and many gin and tonics he would now have to tackle before he and Jim landed back at Heathrow,

***

Back home, Ian was still technically on annual leave. He made the most of it. He took Tolstoy for long walks through North London parks, drank good coffee, strong tea, and baked an apple pie that set off the smoke alarm and singed his hair and beard.

Susan seemed relaxed again, too. She was back to lighting large displays of expensive looking candles and crystals for no apparent reason and reorganising the fridge. She never asked exactly what had happened in Argentina.

"You were gone a while," she said one morning, sipping herbal tea. "Did it all go... alright?"

"There were some complications," Ian said. "But ultimately it all went with a bang in the end."

She smiled, kissed his cheek, and said, "No more bangs for a while please."

"Only the kind that come from baked beans and too much red meat."

They sat in peaceful silence for a moment, before Tolstoy released something unholy from the other side of the kitchen.

"And there it is," said Susan, fanning the air.

Ian added his own loud percussive fart to the kitchen! Shouting "Gunfire." To anyone who might be listening, to celebrate being home.

Susan just shook her head in feigned despair. This was her normality.

When Ian finally returned to the Post Office headquarters, he walked in with a spring in his step, a new tie, and the vague hope that things might go back to...well... normal.

That hope died quickly.

Sebastian van Rooyen – "Seb", to those who had to suffer his company daily – was Ian's new line manager. A small, insect-like man with slicked-back hair, an aggressively narrow chin, and the kind of crisp tailoring that screamed: "I yell at waiters if they don't serve me immediately."

"Ah, Ian," Seb said, extending a limp hand like a Roman senator about to issue a thumbs down. "I've heard... things. But I'm sure you'll prove adequate."

Ian smiled. "I'll aspire to barely functional."

The feeling between them was immediately, visibly mutual.

Seb launched into a droning monologue about "outcome-driven synergy alignment" and "proactive resource interfacing."

Ian made a note: Seb speaks fluent bollocks, word salad, utter twaddle.

Things rapidly deteriorated quickly between them. Seb began issuing pointlessly rigid directives. He also called endless meetings, taking up every waking moment of Ian's time. And then complained nothing ever got done.

"You're expected in the office five days a week. 9 to 5.30. No exceptions."

"Even God rested on the seventh day," Ian said. "You might want to check your contract with the Almighty."

"Your attitude is... problematic," Seb replied.

"Your face is problematic, but here we are," Ian retorted.

It was never going to end well.

The final straw came during a 1-2-1 review with Ian, when Seb, frustrated and flustered, hissed:

"Perhaps the Post Office is no longer the right fit for you."

"Perhaps the world isn't the right fit for your particular brand of mismanagement," Ian replied. "But we can't have it all."

That night, Ian messaged Griffin:

MIGHT HAVE A SLIGHT PROBLEM. AM I ALLOWED TO 'DISAPPEAR' CIVILIANS? I HATE MY NEW BOSS.

Griffin replied:

NO. BUT THERE MAY BE ANOTHER WAY TO MOVE HIM ON IF HE'S GOING TO BE A PROBLEM FOR US. LEAVE IT WITH ME. SO NO 'DISAPPEARING' CIVILIANS PLEASE!

Ian smiled, turned off the secure phone, and poured himself a whisky. Then he walked into the living room, where Susan was curled up with a book and a glass of red wine. He sat beside her, gently took her feet into his lap, rubbing them softly, tenderly.

"I don't know what I did to deserve you," he said softly.

"It's definitely a karmic mishap," she replied, not looking up.

Outside, a barn owl hooted.

Ian stiffened. Birds made him twitchy these days. Particularly birds of prey. But nothing came crashing through the window. No golden eagle. No explosive ceramic dogs.

Just peace.

For now.

Printed in Dunstable, United Kingdom